# The Lost Dog

## el perro perdido

Bryan Kennedy

The Lost Dog
el perro perdido

Copyright © 2015 Bryan Kennedy
Bryan-Kennedy Entertainment, LLC
ISBN 978-0-615-34098-2

Printed in the United States of America

To Choc-Taw: Thank you for fifteen years of unconditional love. We will ride in the truck again someday.

# PROLOGUE

Before now, Monica hadn't really known him. She'd known where he lived, what he liked on his pizza…the kind of toothpaste he used, and the fact he squeezed the tube from the top, the middle, and everywhere that drove her crazy. She'd even known what he wanted to name his first child, boy or girl.

But she hadn't known Jeremy at all growing up, and those years had made him the man he was. Sure, he'd told her where he went to school, and the name of his hometown, but it was a place she had yet to visit, and its memories were ones he'd rather leave behind.

Now they lived in Miami, right in the middle of the melting pot. Its spice mix of different ethnicities bubbled and spat, thousands of people coexisting despite the diversity of their cultures and ideas.

The common denominator among them was a grudging tolerance of the Miami sun. Each dawn it rose with a whisper, then roared like a lion across the sky, until the ground beneath quivered and cracked. The colors of the world grew dusty as it retreated to its cave in the west, and the rich, poor, good, and bad alike emerged from their places of hiding. Rejuvenated, relieved, this was when the people of Miami enjoyed their second wind, and the city transformed into a giant playground.

But Jeremy didn't mind the daytime; the Miami sun was burned into his soul. The beads of sweat on his forehead were as common to him as an old Stetson hat on some long forgotten cowboy.

The faint breeze moving through the terracotta patio did little to stem his perspiration, now dripping down his brow and onto the sandy lashes below.

More often than not the drops were dealt with by a rapid blink of his cool blue eyes, but occasionally the sweat found its way to his nose, where the prominent slope allowed each drop to gain speed and roll right off the tip.

Without thinking he reached for the white undershirt beneath his cheap, button-down work shirt. Grabbing the collar with his right thumb and forefinger, he pulled it up over the bridge of his nose and swiped in a gesture as familiar to him as breathing. Every tee he owned started out with a perfect crew neck, but it only took a few wears to transform them into wrinkled v-necks. Monica had once attempted to break him of the habit, buying him a sleeveless v-neck, and he'd looked at her like she was trying to kill him.

Now it seemed the tables had been turned. He glanced at her lips, her beautiful shoulders, the smooth olive of her complexion. His eyes drifted to the full, dark hair draped to the side of her face, hair he longed to touch.

Jeremy could look anywhere, but her eyes.

Her hand swept through the loose curls, detangling each one with gentle strokes. He'd seen her do it a million times when she was nervous. Unlike Monica, Jeremy was an expert at hiding his emotions, but at that moment his heart was beating so fast he was sure she'd be able to tell. He grabbed his undershirt again and willed himself to meet her gaze, but couldn't.

She sat across from him waiting for him to respond, but he said nothing. Instead of summoning the magic words that might fix it all, he thought of the nights he'd woken to the slap of her hair falling against his face as she collected it at the nape of her neck and slung it over her shoulder. Heavy, thick and sweet as the sun, it would catch in his stubble and tickle his skin, pissing him off to no end. But now it sat beyond his reach, and as the broken words spilled from her lips he couldn't even hear them, could only stare at the long, brown tendrils and wish he could go back in time…soothe the hate and distrust that had become toxic inside her, and prove he was still the man she'd fallen in love with.

The problem was, she'd never really known that man. No one did.

# CHAPTER ONE

The waiter stood politely by their table as he waited for the Jeremy's response, but he was staring across the heads of their family and friends, clearly lost in thought. Monica dismissed the young man with a small, apologetic smile.

Arlo's. This was *their place*.

The place where they'd had their first date, where they'd shared countless conversations about plans for the future, it was even where their wedding reception had been held. Now, it was also the location of a spectacular surprise party, something Jeremy had obviously been planning for some time. Walking through the doors to find all their family and friends waiting, she'd been shocked, but not for the reasons they thought.

No, her disbelief arose from something she didn't dare say out loud. Only Jeremy's best friend Pepe would understand, but he was nowhere to be seen.

Jeremy always took great joy in surprising her. But in the last several hours he had half forgotten about this party himself, and with good reason. When they walked through the doors to the cheers of their friends, he'd jumped so high you'd think she'd been the one to organize it all. In a quiet kind of daze he'd looked around at the balloons and streamers, finally staring at the mariachi band in the corner, where Botista was singing, *"That's Amore"*.

Now they sat together at their own little table, each cloaked in the silence of their overactive brains, forced to smile when another friend or relative sauntered up to congratulate them on their beautiful marriage.

Arlo stood on top of the colorful, tiled bar, and placed his lips to the mouthpiece of an old bugle he blew whenever he got a hundred dollar tip. The note rung out across the chatter and on cue, everyone fell into a hush.

"Friends, tonight we celebrate the most beautiful senora in the world. A surprise from her husband, and not because it is her birthday…"

He paused, sweeping the room with a wide, gleaming grin.

"No! It is not their anniversary, or even the Saint of Valentine's Day. When I asked the handsome detective his reason for this party, he looked at me and said, 'Isn't loving her reason enough?'"

The women sighed, the men cheered, and Monica smiled awkwardly at Jeremy, who continued to stare vacantly beyond her shoulder. *How had it come to this?*

Arlo's smile was like the grill of a sixty-eight Buick, but Monica caught it falter as he glanced in their direction. He paused, as if to see if Jeremy wanted to say a few words, but a faint shake of her head made him turn to the band and wave for them to start again. The party ground on without them.

She was only there because she'd decided that if she had to confront him, a public place would be best. Monica hadn't known all their friends and family would be waiting inside the tinted glass doors. Still, in an odd way their presence comforted her.

Jeremy had never enjoyed talking about himself, or his work. But whenever he offered a small glimpse into that secret life of his, she always listened intently, and refused to back away from the more gruesome details. From time to time he spoke of episodes, escapades and experiences, his thoughts, theories. But for everything he'd told her, he'd left a thousand words unsaid, and now that chasm threatened to swallow them both.

On any other day sitting at 'their table', she would have placed the very tips of her nails atop his hand and slowly traced his veins, as if reading the Braille of his DNA. Once in a while he would try to sneak his hand away to reach for his drink, but she would instinctively wrap her fingers around his wrist and refuse to let him go. Her thirst for his words, attention and touch was so much greater than his need for a drink, and even now, after everything they'd been through, she longed to reach out and grasp him once more. To anchor herself to him, and the world as it had been a week earlier.

Instead she stared at the long, broad hands lying flat on the table, thinking of all they had experienced…and all that she was still yet to find out about.

Glancing around nervously, Monica took a breath and began telling him how she'd thought she knew him better than anyone, despite the fact that he was always able to surprise her. Slowly, painfully, she opened her heart and spilled its blackened contents, finally revealing all that she suspected, and all that she'd discovered. And as the words tumbled from her lips, what had started as detachment froze into stupor, Jeremy pulling further and further away, until he couldn't look at her at all.

Finally they fell into silence once more, Monica's suspicions revealed, and Jeremy's confirmed. The party hummed around them, the company only heightening their solitude, as Monica's heart shattered in into a thousand pieces of love, anger, confusion and compassion. Beneath the disorder she clung to the one thing that seemed bearable. Relief.

# CHAPTER TWO

Her name was Monica Salodimas, and she'd spent the first four years of her life as the only child of Ramos and Maricita Salodimas. The husband and wife owned and operated a very prominent marina in Cabo San Lucas, Mexico, called *Pepita del Azul*. Their brochure boasted a five star rating, and more than the standard service. It provided everything from repairs and rigging, to carpenters, painters and personal valets, a shuffleboard and everything in between.

Pepita del Azul had affectionately been named after Monica, meaning, 'Little Pepper of the Blue', which Monica had been called by her father from when she was still inside her mother's belly. The Salodimas family weren't short on nicknames, Monica's father had one too. To the people around Cabo San Lucas, he was called *'Estes el Hombre'*, or 'This is the Man'.

At fourteen he'd begun to work for Salo Juanes, a millionaire from Cuba and the original owner of the marina, now Ramos' pride and joy. In those days it had been called, Casa del Azul.

To Ramos, Salo had been a kind of god. Well known all over Mexico, South America, and the U.S., Salo surrounded himself with bodyguards, a necessary extension of his power and money. And where one found power and money, one soon discovered millionaires, yachts, women, drugs, passports…and laws being broken faster than they could be upheld.

The marina served as a social tool for Salo Juanes. But, more important than the networking and the parties, Ramos soon discovered it was the legitimate business Salos used to launder his money. As a young man, Ramos saw things around the dock that his intuition warned him never to ask about, and the marina served its purpose off the books, too. Ramos didn't need to be a snoop to realize it was an excellent location for loading and unloading drugs destined for the west coast of the United States.

Salo Juanes seemed to admire Ramos' tight-lipped approach, and while he gave him no special treatment, he did seem to enjoy mentoring him in small ways. He began to teach him everything about the marina world, everything but the drugs and crime, keeping the young man far from that side of the business. He never explained why Ramos was not invited near the glamorous parties, or introduced to the shadier characters, and at first the young man felt disappointed that Salo must distrust him, but as time went on Ramos knew he was not cut out for that lifestyle, and the arrangement suited him fine.

By the time Ramos turned twenty-one years old, he was in full charge of Casa Del Azul and had complete authority over operations. One day Salo started encouraging his daughter, Maricita Maria Monroe Juanes, to spend more time in the office. Hopeless at any task beyond painting her nails, she was still the most beautiful girl Ramos had ever laid eyes on. He had always held a deep yearning for her, like many of the local men who jostled for her attention. But, this was the daughter of Salo Juanes, and no one messed with him, least of all the novice who owed his master so much. Confused, Ramos steered clear of Maricita, even as she flirted relentlessly.

It was months before Ramos realized that Salo had in fact been grooming him for a new role altogether, and that his intentions ran blood deep.

It was a sweltering afternoon when Salo walked into his office and lowered his ample body into the leather chair opposite Ramos'. With characteristic composure, he smiled and announced that both the Feds and U.S. customs were close to making an arrest. His days as a drug lord had come to an end, and he would shortly be indicted and extradited to the United States for trafficking, and sixteen counts of murder.

Ramos gaped at him like a landed fish, finally pulling enough stray thoughts together to urge him to take one of the yachts and disappear. But somehow the older man found the idea of jail preferable to a lifetime of running, which was why he'd been preparing Ramos for a career in the marina business all along. Now he added, it was time for Ramos to step in as the head of his family, also.

Maricita was beautiful, but Ramos had his fair share of admirers too. While his roots sprung from the depths of poverty, this didn't matter to the young girls vacationing in Cabo San Lucas each summer. Needless to say, dreams were crushed all over Casa Del Azul the day Ramos married Maricita.

Shortly after, Salo signed over the business to his son-in-law, and a few weeks later the Feds arrived to cart him off, just as he'd predicted. But when Maricita's father went to prison, things began to change. Ramos spent his days and nights working to keep operations going without the drug money, and Maricita had to work as well. But this time, she wasn't fussing around the office in her bright pink pumps, she was expected to scrub the boats and launder their linens.

When Maricita fell pregnant with their little girl, the happiness returned to their marriage like the sun peeking out from a bank of clouds. She loved the attention she got from Ramos and she really loved not having to wash, scrub, or clean anymore.

She spent her days eating pecan butter scotch ice cream, and wishing for her father to return with his friends…she missed their cigars, whiskey, and their whispered admiration.

Maricita was bored.

# CHAPTER THREE

'The Man' had made quite a name for himself since taking over the newly renamed Pepita del Azul, getting married and now having a child, but running the marina required every spare minute and drop of sweat Ramos could spare. He needed help, but after Maricita had the baby she did not want to talk about returning to work, and when Ramos insisted, she refused to speak to him for weeks.

Pepita del Azul had 230 boat slips, each filled with the newest and the most expensive yachts from all over the world. Millionaires didn't mind paying a pittance of their income for a small tax shelter to dock their third, fourth, or fifth home.

These mega yachts, sail boats and trawlers belonged to high-powered attorneys, Hollywood stars, professional athletes, and CEO's, and when they wanted something, they got it.

Maricita was twenty-nine years old when she decided she was tired of the day-to-day chores and rigors of raising a little girl, but she going to get back on her hands and knees to scrub the decks. She had never seen her mother work a single day in her life, and she so the thought of doing so herself was beyond abnormal.

Maricita was accustomed to being around men with much more money than she and Ramos could ever hope to have, and began to long for the life she'd had growing up, dreaming of men who were powerful, corrupt, and dangerous...like her father.

All little girls grew up listening to fairy tales about maids, saved from poverty by princes who made them their princesses, and Maricita couldn't help feeling her story had been told in reverse. She was young and beautiful, as was her husband, but no fairy godmother could change the fact that the life she was living was beneath her. She hadn't been born for *this*.

At first, she was quite startled by her ability to be deceitful, then she realized it had always lain latent inside her, waiting to come out. It felt comfortable to her, and she grew certain that deceit was in her blood. She could speak both Spanish and English, but few people knew this. She liked to keep it as her little secret and relished the edge it gave her when she got within earshot of gossipmongers, business mergers and drug deals. But most of all, what she loved to hear was the American men who talked about her. She listened their comments about her hair, her eyes, and other parts of her body that were more carnal in nature. At first it made her blush, then it made her feel powerful.

They would often flirt, and she would flutter her lashes at them as if she didn't understand. If she were interested in someone, she would find a way to let them know she knew exactly what they wanted.

Some pretended to be gentlemen, others were truer to their base natures, and grabbed at her as she sauntered past. As she became more adept at the arts of seduction and manipulation she was offered drugs, diamonds and money, and exposed to things she had only heard about, though they seemed unspeakable. So she kept a journal in her head of who said what, who did what, and who had a weakness for beautiful Mexican women.

She had given her father the two things that he wanted; a marriage that he'd picked, and the grandchild he'd wanted. Alas, Monica wasn't a boy, but a girl was better than nothing. And Ramos had done well too, receiving all the benefits of the male heir Salo had never had.

Now, it was time for her to get what *she* wanted.

By the time Monica was three years of age she liked to follow her mother around the marina. Most of the time Maricita seemed fine with this, except when she went aboard one of the larger, shinier boats, with a big silver stripe down its side.

"Not the *Dinero Profunda*," she would say and Monica would wrinkle her brow, wondering what kind of name 'Deep Money' was anyway. Its owner had a low, rolling accent, and liked to speak with her mom in a language she didn't understand.

Early one morning before anyone was up, Maricita and Monica walked the pier towards the boat. It was still dark enough that the lights illuminating the sides of the walkway cast a glow along the worn planks of wood. Monica's mother stopped before the gangplank and leaned down.

"Monica, go and tell your father to hire a new maid," she said.

The little girl looked up, confused to see her mother brush at her eyes, as if she was sad. She wanted to do as she was told, but she felt frozen in place, certain that if she moved something terrible was going to happen.

Maricita repeated the words, then, growing impatient added, "Run along now, hurry. I won't say it again!"

Her head jerked toward the yacht at the rumble of its motor starting, the dark water behind beginning to bubble and fizz. Maricita grabbed her by her shoulders and pointed her towards the marina office.

"Go on, run along."

Monica did as she was told, skipping and jumping to miss every crack she could with her small, bare feet. Her worries were pushed aside as she lost herself in the game, then she turned to see her mother on board the boat as it headed towards the ocean, and guessed they must be having another party.

Her father was where she always found him, sitting in his office, bent over a pile of papers.

"*Estes es el hombre, Estes es el hombre!*"

When Ramos turned his attention to his daughter, she spoke with excitement that bubbled up from inside her, just as the water had.

"Mama says you need a new maid…she's on a boat."

"What?"

Monica paused to check she'd said the words correctly, before repeating them.

"Which boat?" His eyes darted to the tall windows in a way that made her nervous, and together they watched the *Dinero Profunda* slowly head out to sea.

He shook his head, looking like he'd just tasted something bitter.

"What's wrong, Daddy?"

He turned back to her, his dark eyes shining bright as glass, just as her mother's had only a moment before.

"Nothing Pepita. Nothing at all."

# CHAPTER FOUR

Maricita had been right about one thing; Ramos needed to recruit some new help. Not only for the business but for their daughter, who was now without a mother. He could not continue to run his business, be a father *and* a mother to the child.

Ramos prayed for answers, but none came. Eventually, as the work piled up, and as Monica grew increasingly neglected, his thoughts began to grow desperate. His attention turned to a prominent couple who visited the marina often. They were well educated and Ramos had come to know them as good people over the years. Alton and Gloria Howard from Los Angeles, California.

Alton had made his fortune in the development of computer software, recently becoming the controlling shareholder of a major Hollywood film studio. His wife was a professional socialite, but seemed harmless enough.

Ramos liked them both, or at least what he knew of them. He had taken Alton a cigar on the day Monica was born, and Gloria had been the second woman to hold his precious Pepita. She made sure to tell everyone up and down Pepita del Azul that she was in fact the first, and was very proud of the fact Monica had not cried. That night she held Monica saying, "I don't ever want to let her go."

Over the next two years, Alton and Gloria had increased their trips from Los Angeles to Cabo, Gloria trying in vain to convince Alton to move there permanently.

With each visit Gloria had brought little gifts for Monica, and Ramos and Maricita had felt sorry that the woman was incapable of having a child of her own to lavish.

It was a beautiful day when Ramos finished praying. He got up off his knees, gently closing his Bible and placing it on his nightstand. In one hand he clutched his rosary beads, the other opening and then clenching into a fist, as if he couldn't fully grasp the terrible action he'd decided upon.

He began his walk down the pier toward the Howard's yacht with heavy feet, a huge lump in his throat as he continued to roll the beads between his brown, calloused fingers. Ramos had prayed until his mind was numb, fixed upon the image of his small daughter in a dirty shirt, crying for dinner as he stood in the kitchen buttering a burnt piece of toast.

The child needed a mother. The one she'd had, had not been great, but she'd been a lot better than nothing. Monica needed someone who could teach her good things, the right things. A family that could offer her a wonderful education, a life in the United States. He did not want her to grow up and become a servant to the rich people they hosted, or worse, a woman like her mother.

He sat down in front of the Alton's and struggled to think of the best way to say he was offering them his own flesh and blood, his life, his Pepita. Before he could utter a single word, Gloria jumped out of her chair and threw her arms around his neck.

"Yes…yes!"

Tears filled her eyes, her charm bracelets rattled and her expensive makeup began to run down her face. Alton seemed to finally understand what was occurring, and sat back in his chair with a dazed expression. The Hollywood exec had just adopted a Mexican daughter.

Gloria was bouncing around the room, but Ramos' soft voice brought her back to her seat. He conveyed his only request: they were never to tell Monica where she was from, or who her parents were, especially her mother. After a few years when her memories had faded, they could bring her back to Cabo for a holiday and he would admire his child from afar. But she would never know that '*Estes el Hombre*' was her father.

14

This grieved Alton, but he agreed, and told Ramos that if he ever changed his mind to let him know. Alton thought it was better that she at least know her father, but Ramos pleaded with him, explaining that he had prayed about it and that this was the only way.

Monica's roots would not grow in the same toxic soil her mother's had.

# CHAPTER FIVE

His name was Jeremy Harlan, and his habit of stretching out the collar of his t-shirt began at a very early age. It drove his father crazy.

Jeremy was the only child of John Harlan, a war hero and owner of the Harlan Veterinary Clinic in Tampa, Florida. John Harlan might have been a former sergeant in the United States Marines Corp, but no one ever heard the word 'former' leave *his* mouth. He was quick to set someone straight when they made the mistake of speaking of his rank in the past tense, growling, "Once a Marine, always a Marine." His son had heard that phrase at least a thousand times before he'd reached ten years of age.

With no brothers or sisters, Jeremy received the full attention of both his parents. His father raised him with an offensive strategy; it was rumored that he had drawn out an eighteen-year battle plan for the infant before his wife had even arrived at the hospital.

For all his brusqueness Harlan was a commanding man, with good looks and a manner that demanded respect. He had received three Silver Stars by distinguishing himself in multiple acts of heroism. He'd also been awarded two Purple Hearts and the Republic of Vietnam Gallantry Cross medal. Unlike many others who came back from the conflict, Jeremy's dad was quick to talk about his encounters during the war. He knew those medals were not of any use to him left rotting in a jungle somewhere; he had paid the price for them, and they would serve him well.

Born and raised in Eastern Tennessee, Harlan had one goal as a child: to grow up and play college football. But he didn't want to play football just anywhere. No, he was going to play at the University of Tennessee for the 'Vols', the Volunteer's.

In high school he'd been the quarterback, and trained harder than any one of his coaches had ever seen. During his senior year, he'd received a letter of recruitment that left his hands trembling, but it wasn't from 'The Big Orange'. This envelope bore the stamp of an eagle and an anchor; the United States Marine Corps. John Harlan may never have played football for UT, but he did serve his country during Vietnam.

When he returned home from battle he enrolled at the University of Tennessee in Knoxville, where he obtained a BA in business and graduated at the top of his class. With his undergraduate degree he applied to the College of veterinary medicine at UT, and was readily accepted.

Again, Harlan was at the top of his class, standing out everywhere he went and in whatever he set his mind to. Not many men, much less the other students, had experienced anything close to what Harlan had in Vietnam. They hadn't taken a bullet in their thigh, or walked around with shrapnel imbedded in their shoulder. For him, sitting through eight hours of classes was a holiday.

Many of his classmates at the University had protested against the war, but they never made a peace sign in front of Harlan, and he took no shame in the fact that he was a Vietnam vet. Instead, he wore his service on his sleeve like the tattoo inked into his chest. He'd got it after being shot, a four-inch bull's-eye located right over his heart. He loved that tattoo, and he never passed up an opportunity to shed his shirt, lying by the lake, or throwing a ball on the university lawn.

Other men were not like him; they allowed themselves to be weak and always gave up so easily. Harlan walked tall and proud, and he had become very good at separating himself from others, including those closest to him.

Jeremy's mother tried to tell her husband not to be so hard on their son. He wasn't a seventeen-year-old man going off to war, he was just a little boy wanting to throw a ball with his daddy. But John would say, "A man is made from the day he's born. When my son is called to fight, to defend himself, his country and his family, he won't be scared of throwing a punch, or pulling a trigger."

Jeremy's mother knew better than to risk his anger by arguing. Still, she wept at his words. They weren't raising Jeremy to be a man, but a Marine.

# CHAPTER SIX

Growing up in Tampa provided an excellent environment for an athletic young boy, the climate allowing for year-round sports. Jeremy spent his days in school and his afternoons at practice.

Like his father, he was a natural at everything he applied himself to. His room was covered with posters of famous football, basketball and baseball players, and the shelves were lined with so many trophies that when the sun hit at a certain angle, visitors risked being blinded just by walking through the door.

The only thing that looked out of place in a boy's bedroom was the Marine footlocker at the end of Jeremy's bed. His dad had made him build it when he was eight, and together they had painted on the lid;

*Jeremy Jacob Harlan*
*Son of Sgt. John Harlan*
*United States Marine Corps*
*Hoo-Rah!*
*Semper Fi... Do or die.*

His father had beamed upon the box with pride, but Jeremy's smile was one born from years of practice; countless mornings spent folding his clothes into perfect squares, or making his bed with surgical precision. But his least favorite activity came at night, when he polished his shoes. The task itself was simpler than attempting the perfect crease on a Sunday shirt, but the shoes were the only activity they did as a father-son activity. The man took great pleasure in pointing out missed spots or a frayed lace, until the boot was clenched so tightly in Jeremy's hand it took all his self control not to hurtle it out the window. Needless to say, Jeremy got away with very little at home.

So, he began to push the envelope at school.

Tradition dictated that each player on the basketball team had to steal an underclassman's basketball shoes, lace them together and toss them over a beam in the gymnasium's ceiling. For the rest of the season they would annoyingly dangle above their owner's head. But no one had ever dared to do this to the coach's shoes, at least not until Jeremy Harlan gathered all his teammates on the court before practice.

Coach Michaels arrived that day in his street shoes and gym shorts. As the team ran through their drills, the thump of dribbling balls was accompanied by barely suppressed laughter, particularly when the players worked on their in-bound passes underneath the south end goal. The laughter grew, the coach having no idea his shoes were hanging right above his head. Jeremy lobbed around the court with a light smile, the picture of innocence.

At the end practice it came time for the team to run sprints. Coach Michaels blew his whistle and yelled, "All right, everyone on the baseline!"

Taking their positions on the north-end, the players readied themselves for what they called 'suicides'.

The coach yelled for Tiny, the team's manager, to put ten minutes on the scoreboard. Tiny weighed in at 280 pounds and would have given anything to play, but his considerable mass did not allow for quick movement. He had learned to be happy filling water bottles and handing out towels, especially when Jeremy asked him for one; he had a special blue towel just for him. He thought of Jeremy as a friend, and that made him *a somebody*.

On this particular day he had purposely left the scoreboard off to reduce any attention to the black leather loafers dangling beneath it. When Coach Michaels yelled out again, Tiny sat at the scorers' table staring down at the control board, a violent flush spreading across his cheeks.

All the players froze, waiting to see what would happen next. His fifteen-year-old brain had good intentions, but like most adolescent boys, didn't think things through to their rational conclusion. If only Tiny had turned on those little lights, they might have been all the coach had noticed. Instead, his stare was locked in the direction of his shoes, waiting for the board to come on. The entire group hung in anticipation, watching as his eyes slowly drifted downward, only to widen momentarily, then harden.

He bit into his whistle, and every player could see the muscles in his jaw tighten. He stared in silence for what seemed like eternity, before he finally ground out, "Who?"

Predictably, this was met with complete silence.

With a slight tick of the eye, he informed the boys they would run suicides until someone came clean, or until no one was left standing. But when he blew that whistle, his eyes were set on Jeremy Harlan.

If it had been anyone but Jeremy, someone on the team would have tattled. But the other players were afraid of him, and knew that even 'suicides' were better than suffering the alternative behind Pizza Hut on a Friday night.

Coach Michaels watched as the team ran and ran, until eighteen boys lay sprawled across the gym floor. Some were curled near puddles of vomit, others flat on their backs, moaning. But amidst the coughs, cries and panting came the soft pad of two sneakers, squeaking as they reached the line and turned against the polished timber floor.

Coach Michaels knew he could not run Jeremy long enough or hard enough to make him quit, so he sent Tiny to the coaches' office to get the paddle. Tiny couldn't meet Jeremy's eye upon returning, thrusting the object at the coach before lumbering away.

Jeremy, barely standing, walked over and placed his hands upon his knees, chest heaving with each breath. When the punishment didn't come, he stood.

Coach Michaels handed him the paddle.

"You're gonna take this home, and hand it to you father."

Jeremy looked away before the man could see the surprise, and terror, on his face.

"Yes, sir."

# CHAPTER SEVEN

Monica knew that at the end of the municipal parking lot she had a chance at finding a good spot. Unfortunately, it meant passing the construction workers at the soon-to-open downtown office of the Los Angeles County Bank.

She was well accustomed to being whistled at by blue collar guys, as well as businessmen in expensive suits, from time to time. She paid the catcalls no mind, but she did make an effort to avoid them if she could. She just wanted a parking space in front of the library.

*So where could a lost girl park?*

She said it to herself by habit. It had become some sort of silly game she enjoyed playing from when she was younger, back when she had just gotten her driver's license. Monica would never forget the power she felt the day she held that small card and realized a new world awaited. A world she shared with her best friend, Shelly Weiser, whom she'd been close to since preschool.

Monica and Shelly often referred to the children at The New Knowledge Learning & Development Center as victims, casualties of parents wanting the nuclear family, without having to deal with the associated inconveniences.

This included dropping their children off in the mornings. For one thing, it required getting out of bed, bathing, and having the hairdresser perfect their effortless up-dos. If their nails weren't done and they had to wave at someone, well, best to go with no greeting at all. Some things we more trouble than they were worth.

# The Lost Dog

Monica remembered her mother, Gloria, getting stuck with the task one Monday morning. She had fired their nanny a day too soon and had no one to take Monica to school. Gloria had encouraged Monica to simply stay at home, or venture out in the afternoon for some shopping and a movie. A ten year old Monica had beamed in excitement.

"Just you and me, Mom?"

Gloria's eyes widened in surprise.

"No Pepper, baby."

Gloria either could not, or would not, ever say the name *Pepita*—though Alton sometimes called her that. She liked it, though she couldn't for the life of her guess why her parents had come up with such a name.

"I have things to do, but you can go all by yourself, with Emit of course." Emit was Gloria's driver.

When Monica started crying Gloria begrudgingly agreed to take her to school, the ten minute drive preferable to five hours in a mall somewhere.

Monica was proud to have her mother personally drop her off, and hoped the other children might see them. As soon as Gloria pulled into the car line she began smiling at the very few parents she knew, and their younger personal assistants—none of whom she knew, except for those she'd hired and fired.

Gloria's smile was a careful study in restraint, not enough to cause future wrinkles, or reveal the new one near her left eye. From the corner of her grimace she spoke to Monica as if she were hosting a gossip segment on TV.

"Oh, Pepper baby, look at her hair and makeup! Someone was in a rush this morning."

She gave a stiff wave to a passing Japanese couple, and Monica smiled at their son, who was a friend of hers.

"Always so uptight and proper! Do those people wear *anything* other than golfing attire?"

A sick feeling grew inside Monica's stomach as she wondered if she was one of "those people". She wished she had gone to the movie with Emit. Emit never said a word about anyone. In fact, he never spoke at all.

The car inched forward, and Monica already had her little hand on the door latch, unable to get out fast enough.

"With some luck I'll have another assistant by tomorrow, or Emit can work a double—"

Monica was out the car door and looking for Shelly before the woman could finish.

The first time Monica and Shelly's families met was when each girl asked their parents if they might invite the other to their birthday party. Each family sent the other a token invitation out of courtesy, and thus discovered the girls were born on the same day.

Each year Gloria would say to Alton, "Why did you have to pick the 1st for Monica's birthday?"

Alton and Maggie could not remember the exact day Monica had been born, and while a phone call to her father would have rectified the situation, Gloria didn't want any details that tied the girl to her prior identity. It was bad enough that Alton had insisted she keep the name Monica.

Years passed without a single birthday, until Monica eventually began to question why she was the only child she knew that didn't have one. As usual, it was Monica's 'personal assistant' Amber, who went to bat for her. She approached Alton and informed him that Monica needed a specific date to celebrate her appearance in the world.

Alton readily agreed, helped no doubt by some of Amber's more persuasive assets, and decided on January 1st, based mostly on the fact that he loved being number one. And so Monica finally had her birthday.

# CHAPTER EIGHT

At ten Monica was told by her mother that she was old enough to wear makeup, and that she should start wearing it soon. Gloria ordered her assistant to visit Rique, who was her personal hair and makeup consultant. She wanted Monica to be made over as he saw appropriate, preferably a little paler, and minus the unruly brows.

With that in mind Gloria arranged a surprise for Monica when she returned home from her first beauty consultation. She told her assistant specifically what products to buy and how to arrange them on Monica's new gift: a six-foot tall antique cherry wood makeup table. It included five large mirrors, all framed with the same lights they used in the actors' trailers at Alton's studio.

When Monica returned they headed up the stairs, the little girl already disappointed. She had always wanted a pony and she knew there wouldn't be one upstairs. She still held out for hope for a kitten or a puppy, but that was starting to seem like a long shot too.

When she saw the table, she didn't even realize it was the gift. She continued to search her suite for something that looked wrapped, or something with a bow.

When Amber pointed to the table, Monica's confusion was obvious. She had grown up seeing her mother sit in front of a table just like this one, the only difference being that her mom's was made out of marble.

Amber smiled. She knew Monica was not in the least bit interested in makeup, or anything her mother endorsed.

On Monica and Shelly's sixteenth birthday, they were next in line at the Department of Motor Vehicles to get their photos taken. Monica had waited for what seemed like forever for the day to finally come. Shelly was sitting next to her with the contents of her purse spread out over her lap, half of it spilling onto the linoleum floor.

There were tubes of lipstick, lip-gloss, powder, eyeliner, eye shadow, colored glitter, hair ties, and several options for earrings—but only one matching pair.

She was thinking over what style to go for in her photo and would not stop talking about it.

Monica laughed. "Why are you so worried about that stuff, Shell?"

As her friend divulged the many reasons one did not want to be attached to a bad license photo for years on end, Monica thought about what this moment really meant, beyond a silly photo. To finally get her driver's license and have the freedom to 'be gone'; the liberation of it was overwhelming.

School was boring. Monica made straight A's and never studied. She could have any guy she wanted; they all wanted her. She would try to talk to them, and found their awkward fumbling of words intriguing, but even that novelty quickly wore thin.

But to hit the open highway and drive, the wind in her hair and everything and nothing laid out before her. Her body trembled in anticipation.

# CHAPTER NINE

*Pop!*

The flash went off at the same time the bubble between Monica's lips exploded in a sticky mess across her cheek.

Popping bubblegum was a habit Monica had developed at a very early age. For years now she was completely unaware that she even purchased gum, much less chewed it constantly. She was always popping tiny little bubbles that would come and go as quickly as she blinked.

The photo lady looked at the computer screen with a vague expression of disgust. "I guess you're gonna want another one, huh?"

Monica jumped up, peeling off the gum and popping it back in her mouth. "Nope, but thank you."

In fact, when the lady showed her the photo on her monitor, Monica insisted on keeping it, picturing Gloria's face when she pulled the card from her wallet. "Yes ma'am that is just fine."

The more she looked at it, the better she liked it. Her large brown eyes stared at the camera in a slight look of surprise, the pink gum hanging from her face like a gruesome skin infection. Shelly begged her to take another, but Monica smiled as she waited for the lamination process.

"Eww, Monica. You can't hand that to a bouncer at a club! Take another one."

"No."

The lady handed her license to her, smiled and yelled, "Next!"

Monica popped four quick bubbles as she headed for the door, like an outlaw shooting his gun in the air after being run out of town.

"I can't seem to find a place to park?"

It had been six years since the gum incident, and newly out of college Monica had learned so much. One of the most important lessons: That all she had to do to find a parking space was sit with her palms on the steering wheel, hide her true expression behind a pair of sunglasses, and just say the magic words…"I can't seem to find a place to park?"

And *poof,* the lot attendant appeared.

He approached Monica nervously, straightening his tie and reaching around to stuff his excess shirttail back into his waistband.

"Can I help you?"

She took her right hand, and with her long fingers and perfect nails, raised her glasses just above her forehead. Wrinkling her nose, she squinting her eyes at the sun just enough to be cute. Then she said the magic words.

"I can't seem to find a place to park?"

Funny, there always happened to be a car parked directly in front of her that the attendant just so happened to have the keys on hand for.

As she exited her BMW in shorts, flip-flops, and as always chewing gum, she smiled and said, "Oh thanks so much. I'll only be a few minutes." Then she walked off to her destination, the public Library.

When it came time to leave the attendant finally got up the nerve to speak to her on a non-parking related subject.

"Read any good books lately?"

A flush spread across his cheeks as he heard the stupidity of his own words. It was almost cute.

"No," Monica replied, as he opened her door and watched her slip her long legs into the car. He shut the door and leaned against it, resting his hands on the top of the hood.

"Are you meeting your boyfriend here?"

Monica looked straight ahead and then over her right shoulder as she slipped her sandals off, pushed the clutch in with her bare foot, and put the car in reverse.

"I don't have a boyfriend." She said it with the slightest smile, not wanting to be too cold and risk their comfortable arrangement.

"Would you like a boyfriend?" the attendant fired back, seizing his window of opportunity. "I mean…uh, would you like to buy me a drink? I mean, do you drink?"

He gaped at her, the words continuing until he looked like he was ready to clamp a hand over his own mouth.

"Perhaps?"

She started backing up, and he lost his balance for a moment when his hands failed to relay the message to his brain to move his feet. Monica stopped for a brief moment, allowing him the chance to let go or risk being dragged across the parking lot.

"What are you reading in there all day?"

She sighed. "I'm studying trees."

He was attempting to regain his balance, and control his wayward mouth at the same time.

"Trees?"

"Uh huh."

As the car moved away once more he cried out, "I'm a tree hugger too!" He started to tell her he went to Berkley, but his words were lost to the growl of her engine as she pulled away.

"Tree hugger," she snorted, flooring the accelerator. "Not sure you can hug a family tree."

# CHAPTER TEN

Jeremy might have driven the faculty at Pasco County High School to their wit's end, but most of his misdemeanors were forgiven for his athletic ability; the boy was in trouble as often as he was in the end zone. But his antics on and off the field meant Jeremy was destined to end up in a uniform—athletic or otherwise.

John Harlan told everyone, beginning with the doctor who delivered him, that one day they would see Jeremy wearing the jersey of a University of Tennessee football player, or the collared jacket of a United States Marine. But by the time that baby had grown into an adolescent, most of the town thought an orange jumpsuit would be closer to the mark.

There were several times Jeremy came close, and on each occasion he was met with the meaty, weathered face of Police Chief Ronnie Roland.

Chief Roland was a major influence on young Jeremy, but not by choice or desire. He'd attended the University of Tennessee alongside Jeremy's father, and both played on the Pasco County High football team before one had gone to war, the other to play for Knoxville.

There wasn't a tougher nose guard than Ronnie Roland. He'd played four years at UT, and then six with the Tampa Bay Buccaneers, before moving to Tampa to run for police chief in his first year away from the NFL. His popularity in the Tampa area was such that he hardly had to campaign. Ronnie Roland was tough, street smart, and a good man.

And most likely the only one who knew both sides of Jeremy Harlan.

# The Lost Dog

Like most, Roland knew the Jeremy who'd broken every record for the most rushing yards and the most passing yards, in a single season of his freshman year, only to break them again the year after.

But he also knew about all the records that had been kept quiet from the public, too. Jeremy had broken several minor—and some not-so-minor—laws, that resulted in Jeremy obtaining the kind of record Roland best suppressed, at least for the time being.

The boy was the only son of Sgt. John Harlan, and for all his father's medals and awards, Chief Roland knew the man wasn't about to win any accolades for parenting.

It was the August before Jeremy's senior year, when the teenager was brought in to Pascoe County Jail in the early hours of a Saturday morning. He'd been charged with vandalism, breaking and entering.

He sat in the usual chair across from Chief Roland's desk. It was empty.

Jeremy had seen the inside of Roland's office so many times that he could recite every trophy Roland had received in high school and college, and every word inscribed upon them.

Sitting there was ceremonial; Jeremy knew Chief Roland would go easy on him and even though this was one of his worst offences, he guessed Roland would quickly send him home. The greatest punishment wasn't the older man's tough words, but the torture of having to sit and stare at all that UT orange. Tennessee football photos and a UT jersey was framed and showcased behind Roland's chair. There were pictures of Neyland Stadium filled to capacity…and his least favorite item in the room, a droopy eared bobble-headed dog, the team mascot *Smokey*.

Jeremy reached out with his finger and tapped the head of the dog; only to set off its tinny recording:

*Rocky top you'll always be,*
*Home sweet home to me,*
*Good 'ole Rocky Top…*

It kept playing and playing, and Jeremy grabbed it, trying to find the off switch. He hated that song, he really hated it…but couldn't find the switch, so he grabbed the dog's head and twisted it off.

He sat, holding the head in one hand and what was left of its body in the other, as the song groaned out its final bars.

As the door opened and closed behind him, he shoved the head into his left pocket, the body in his right, and tried to look neutral. Chief Roland walked around him and sat down, his old chair squeaking from the strain.

There was no way the man sitting before him could have fit into the framed jersey on the wall. That sent his eyes drifting down to the half-deflated footballs signed by people like Johnny Majors, Condredge Holloway, Bobby Majors, and Willie Gault. He had never heard of any of them, and thought, who cares? It wasn't that he hated those players, rather that he hated the fact they'd played for Tennessee.

# CHAPTER ELEVEN

The angry squeak from Chief Roland's chair snapped Jeremy out of his thoughts, right before the man's words did. Unfamiliar words. Apparently he was through letting Jeremy "off the hook".

"Look here, son. I know what you've suffered." He paused, his tone softening. "My old man used to beat me too."

Jeremy looked away, trained his eyes on a poster in the opposite corner.

"I know the signs, and I know your dad. Hell I know him better than anyone. I know what he's capable of."

This was a more direct approach than the Chief generally took, and Jeremy was surprised to feel a hot pressure behind his eyes. The older man pressed on.

"I believe I could tell you all about it, could describe exactly what he does to you. Shit, the whole department could. I went to school with the son of a bitch."

*Son of a bitch*. When the Chief said that Jeremy made eye contact with Roland for a split second. It wasn't easy to hate Chief Roland, and deep down Jeremy knew the man understood him. *But then why didn't he lift a damn finger to stop it?*

The thought was loud in his head, so loud he wondered if Roland could hear it. He dropped his eyes to the floor again.

"I was an all-American at Tennessee my senior year."

Jeremy rolled his eyes, Chief Roland getting up and walking around his desk to stand before him, toe to toe.

"And, you know, I played for the Buc's for a few years. I was what you young ones would call a 'badass'. But still, bad as I thought I was, there was always someone who could make me look like a pussy, right?"

Jeremy stared at the worn eel skin boots and wondered where the hell this was going.

"Well, this one guy showed up around from time to time who I would never tangle with, and I had my chance. Plenty of 'em."

The chief paused and the boots stretched as he shifted back on his heels.

"That one guy was your daddy, John Harlan."

*Great*, thought Jeremy.

"Our linebacker coach, Coach Spencer, saw him in an intramural basketball game with ex-service men, scrimmaging the basketball team up at UT. Coach Spencer couldn't believe what he saw, said Harlan was one of the most gifted athletes he'd come across."

Jeremy felt the man's stare beating down upon the top of his head, but his eyes refused to lift and meet it. The whole thing felt like some sort of trick, where he had to sit in the Chief's office surrounded by every icon, emblem, and sticker touting the one place he hated—his dad's alma mater. If that weren't enough, he had to listen to heroic stories about the asshole, too.

*Thunk!*

Chief Roland's size-13 boot slammed into Jeremy's chair.

"Paying attention, boy?"

Jeremy looked up.

"Coach Spencer tried and tried to get your dad to play football, to join our team. Word got around pretty fast to all of us players, and we began to pray, especially ol' Marcus."

The chief laughed as he backed away from Jeremy a bit.

"We weren't praying that Coach would succeed in getting him to play...No sir, we were praying he'd fail. No one wanted to go up against Harlan every day in practice, cause of what happened in a bar off campus one night.

"It was down on the strip, my senior year. We were drinking beer and just hanging out, a bunch of us players. We thought we owned the place, and pretty much did. If someone walked in that door and they weren't a football player, they usually took their buttoned-down, khaki-wearing candy-ass back to their dorm. We liked it that way. It was sort of an unwritten law.

He had Jeremy's attention, and smiled.

"We had just gotten back from beatin' Ole Miss down there in Oxford, and were out on the strip for a little celebration, you know… I guess half the team was in there.

"Well, several pitchers had been emptied, and that's when I heard the crash… and out of the corner of my eye I instantly see two or three our D-linemen making their way towards the sound.

"The music was loud, and to tell you the truth, the beer had me in such a state that I really didn't seem to care too much. Mostly because I'd seen that one of the guys heading towards the ruckus was Marcus Waller.

"Marcus was our left defensive tackle, he played right next to me, and later got drafted in the first round to Pittsburgh. Marcus was only six-two, but he would have been at least six-five if he had a neck. His legs were as big as tree trunks, and he weighed two hundred and ninety-five pounds. That's big today, but back then it was huge."

Roland's eyes danced at the memory.

"I thought to myself that whatever happened would stop very quickly, once Marcus got over there. So I sat back to enjoy the show," he said, tucking his thumbs inside the front of his gun belt.

"I was thinking it was some frat-rat in the wrong place at the wrong time…probably hooking up with some debutant beauty queen that had caught the eye of one of our guys."

Chief Roland let out a laugh.

"Well, the noise got louder, and louder, and I could see more of my buddies running in that direction. I heard my name hollered a few times…figured I better head over and check it out." He squinted both eyes, transported back to the excitement of the night. "I couldn't see much as I walked into the mayhem. But as I got closer, I caught glimpses of a body; a chiseled body…looked like it was carved from rock.

"Some of the best fights I've ever seen have been between football players. But then…but then I saw something that told me this was different. I saw a fist, and then another, and each time it was connecting with a different target, fired out like a missile.

"And then I knew he definitely wasn't one of us, by the tattoo…"

He paused, looking into Jeremy's eyes as his fat finger drew a circle around his heart.

"It was a bull's-eye, right here, daring the world to just try and take him."

Jeremy looked away. He'd seen that tattoo enough times; he didn't need some fat cop to tell him all about it.

"Yeah son, I ain't never seen nothing like it. After your dad had cleared the first wave, the second wave was a little slower to commit, if you know what I mean. And that included me. It was nasty. A lot of blood and torn clothing, worse than any bust up here in Pasco County.

"And then I saw it, poor 'ol Marcus lying on the floor face down, like he'd stopped to take a nap…He was out cold."

Roland sunk onto the edge of his desk, as if he'd just gone a round himself.

"I was one of the ones who tried to calm things down and it took a while for the team to settle, but your dad, hell, he was fine. Not a hair out of place…he wasn't even out of breath. He just stood there with his shirt torn open, his eyes scanning the room, waiting. It was like he was taking inventory, sizing up each possible enemy, dividing them into classes by height, reach, weight, you know… he was freaky like that. Still is if you ask me.

"We asked him if we could pick up our wounded. He nodded slightly, and it took a while but we got everyone up. Well, all but Marcus. He was too heavy to lift, so we just eased around your dad and rolled him over so he could breathe.

"Me, I went back to my pitcher of beer, and John Harlan sat down and went back to his, with Marcus sleeping at his feet."

# CHAPTER TWELVE

"Enough about your asshole dad."

Chief Roland folded his huge forearms across his chest.

"You know I'm gonna have to send an officer to go knock on your daddy's door today and tell him someone broke into his clinic. Can't keep that from happening."

He shook his head, a large frown of creasing his reddened face. "We have to tell him some *sicko* put a bunch of mouse traps through all his cages, and that a lot of pissed off clients are gonna come pick up their kitties, only to find them worse off than when they left them."

He'd pushed off the table again and was pacing back and forth in front of Jeremy.

"All those poor cats with mousetraps hangin' off of 'em." He stopped pacing.

"Jeremy, you know what your dad will do to the person who did this, don't you?"

Only silence filled the room.

Hours earlier Jeremy had let himself in the backdoor of his dad's clinic. He carried a pack with about ten mousetraps and a larger rattrap.

Getting caught was certainly not part of his plan. His intended to be at home and in bed when the phone call came, or the knock on the door.

He was careful inside the clinic, light on his feet and moving swiftly. His idea was to place mousetraps inside the cages, being careful not to let the cats escape, or to spring the traps across his own fingers. He had just gotten the first cage door closed, and was opening the second, moving quickly.

*Snap!*

He turned to look towards the noise, the excitement rushing through his body like volts of electricity.

*Snap! Snap!*

He couldn't take his eyes off of the cage he had just closed, while his hands fumbled with the latch of the cage now in front of him.

*SNAP!*

There went the rattrap, and a large *yeow* soon followed. His plan was working better than he had ever imagined, and he hurried ahead, setting trap after trap and placing them two in each cage. As the traps went off the meowing soon turned to howling. The animals weren't seriously injured, but they were pissed enough to give his dad a serious headache in the morning.

Jeremy stood back to take in his masterpiece. He thought he'd been careful, going so far as to clad his hands in plastic gloves, but he'd forgotten to close the blinds his dad left open at night. A good Samaritan had called the Sheriff's Department after seeing a dark figure prowling around long after closing hours, and minutes later an officer arrived just as he'd been leaving.

The police chief was right, his dad was gonna kill him.

But, deep down Jeremy had known this day was bound to come. Hadn't he been courting disaster for so long, because for some sick reason, he wanted it to happen? It had only been a matter of time.

He might not kill him per se, but Jeremy knew his dad was capable of doing so, he'd come very close to crossing that line before. Sometimes he wished the bully had gone ahead and done it. Would certainly have spared him the trouble he now found himself in.

Chief Roland was now standing back behind his desk, still talking.

"I'm gonna make a deal with you, boy."

He reached into his back pocket and took out a green can of Skoal. Opening the lid, he grabbed a pinch and placed it in the bottom center of his lip, then wiped his fingers on his pants, before offering it to Jeremy.

Jeremy still had both of his hands in his letterman jacket. He moved his right hand around the body of *Smokey* and pulled out his own can, copying the Sheriff's routine.

Roland smiled, probably glad he hadn't been made to share.

Digging in bottom right drawer of his desk, Roland fished out two Styrofoam cups. Nothing special about them, except that they weren't used for drinking. An old Burger King sack in the trashcan failed to produce any napkins, so Roland wadded up some torn newspaper and placed it inside each cup, then handed the closest to Jeremy.

"If you keep your end of my proposal Jeremy, I'll write the report myself."

He paused to spit into his cup.

"Ya hear?"

Jeremy didn't respond, unwilling to agree before the more details were revealed. The bitter tobacco melted its way around his mouth.

"I'll put down in my report that someone saw some Hispanic boy run out your dad's clinic, leaving town before any of us could stop him. Might even mention a spate of animal related crimes right through the state, make it more believable." Roland's eyebrows were raised, as if to emphasize the full value of his offer. "I'll tell my boys to go to their graves with it, and personally make sure they do."

He spat into his cup again.

"All you have to do, is keep your nose clean this summer and on into the fall during football season. But, the minute you screw up again, I will crack this case, and that Hispanic boy will suddenly become a six-foot, blue eyed, juvenile delinquent. Comprendomento?"

Jeremy sat, stoic and silent, waiting for *the real deal*. There was no way Roland would go to this much trouble, just to keep him out of it. The chief sat back in the chair, apparently waiting for some sign from Jeremy.

"Is that it?" he asked, knowing that it wasn't.

"Nope, that ain't all of it."

He leaned forward with his elbows on the desk. "Now, this is just between you and me, son. If anyone else hears what I am about to say, I will lose my job, and you will have to face your dad on your own."

Jeremy nodded.

"I'll let you walk out of here right now, with no police record whatsoever. Understand? None."

Jeremy nodded again.

"I'll even go back to your first bust and get rid of that, as well as the five or so that came after."

He scooted even closer, swallowing the spit in his mouth and dropping to a whisper.

"You remember that Coach Bradford from Tennessee? The one's been calling and trying to recruit you?" His voice got a little more aggressive. "The one you told thirty times 'there ain't no way in hell I'll ever go to UT'? The same coach you told you'd sign with *any* team that played against them, just so you could kick their asses?"

Roland's face was red. Clearly he needed to spit, but he was angry and his throat bobbed as he swallowed again.

"Well, that same coach is going to call you tomorrow, I'd say...about eight in the morning? And you're gonna be up waiting on that call."

A huge smile crossed Chief Roland's face. A 'check mate' grin that made Jeremy want to put his fist through a wall. Shoulders slumped, he realized that this deal was one he'd probably have to take. He'd wanted to dance with the devil, but the thought of answering for his latest prank sent a cold prickle down his spine.

He looked up at Roland and gave a short, stiff nod. But instead of looking pleased, the fat mess was looking at the table, perplexed.

"Now where the hell's Smokey got to?"

# CHAPTER THIRTEEN

After five years of marriage, Monica had a routine.

This day was no different. It was humid, and the dew still glistened on the petals of her favorite flowers, green Gerber daisies, cut fresh from the garden. She began to arrange them in a vase at the kitchen counter, where she liked to sit on a stool and read while Jeremy was sleeping.

She loved the mornings with her flowers and of course, Grady. Always in a good mood, the four-year-old chocolate Labrador Retriever was beyond spoiled. Every morning he waited for Monica to get up, and by the time she had, would be standing by the door poking his nose at the leash hanging from its hook. Monica would take him for a walk, and then he'd return to the patio and lie in the corner to catch some shade and enjoy the wet tiles where Monica had watered her garden.

Usually she would wait at least an hour before waking Jeremy. She didn't mind the wait much; Grady kept her distracted enough. Still, she would think of Jeremy while she dug around in the potting soil, planting. Sometimes she would stop what she was doing, stand in the doorway and stare at her husband as he slept in their bed. He was an enigma to her, exerting a relentless magnetic pull that drew her closer, but never deep enough.

It comforted her a great deal to know that he was home safe, just inside the double French doors leading out to her garden. It was important to her to let him rest. Monica knew his work sometimes kept him away from home till the wee hours of the morning, and she feared that if he got too fatigued, he might get sloppy and fail to protect himself.

Just the week prior he'd called to tell her that he'd landed a heavy case, and wouldn't be home for a while. Discouraged, she did her best to hide her disappointment, popping a bubble so that Jeremy would think she was just fine.

She'd told him she loved him and hung up, looking out at the ocean and feeling lonely. Then, half an hour later, the door opened and Jeremy appeared with a bouquet of roses, and a bottle of wine. She leapt into his arms, taking in his scent, his warmth, his strength.

"You lied to me!" she cried into his throat.

"No," he laughed. "I've got a case, but I couldn't stand that sound in your voice." He pulled her even closer. "I'll work on the file later tonight."

Even after years of marriage, he never failed to surprise her, doing exactly the thing she least expected.

Problem was, sometimes she felt like she didn't know which way was up. It was like there was this whole aspect to his life she knew nothing about. Sometimes he would talk to her about his assignments, but more often Jeremy seemed reluctant to discuss the work he was involved in.

Monica was careful not to push, but it took every grain of self control not to grasp him by his shirt and shake the answers right out of him. She wanted desperately to know him, to help, to comfort, to be his wife in everything.

Instead she'd pop one of her little bubbles, smile, and put her arms around his tanned neck to give him a warm, gentle kiss. Then she would look into his eyes with that look… her look. The look that was sought by many men, but belonged to him, and only him.

And he would gaze at her, his face cast in a mixture of love and awe and something else…fear, fleeting and easy to miss, but there. It made her heart clench for him, and she knew that some part inside him wanted to open up to her, and that one day it might happen. But always that fear returned, hinting at secrets too great for him to face, or too painful for her to bear.

# CHAPTER FOURTEEN

She thought to leave the water in the bathroom running, to make him think she had forgotten to turn it off. He would stagger into the bathroom to turn off the faucet, probably wearing only his boxer briefs. She loved seeing him like that, drawn to his athletic build, his shoulders, even the scar from his shoulder surgery.

She imagined greeting him with a soft "Good morning, baby," before he pulled her into his arms and pressed his lips against her throat.

Monica was already halfway to the bathroom when her conscience kicked in and she paused.

*Let him sleep.*

Instead she turned around to ready the coffee machine. She would get the paper from the front door and keep busy until she heard the telltale sound of the toilet flush.

It made her feel silly to admit the small flutter it sent through her stomach. She would giggle and wonder how she'd become so pathetic, especially after so many years of living with the man.

Their little beach condo, a very generous wedding gift from Alton, was the centre of their happy life together. Monica had painted the French doors from their bedroom a bright blue, and the walls in avocado green and butter yellow. The blue trim seemed to frame the view outside, making Monica feel as if she lived inside a beautiful postcard.

She had proudly laid the burnt orange tiles on the patio herself, and all along the aluminum railing hung window boxes full of snapdragons, daisies, marigolds, impatiens and dahlias. And lights! Little white lights wrapped around the taller trees and plants, and at least two hundred strung across the patio roof, forming a starry canopy above their heads.

Sometimes, sitting outside with Grady, she would notice big yachts off in the distance that would give her an odd sense of comfort. Odd, in that Alton and Gloria had disliked all water related activities, and she hadn't set foot on board a boat until she was well into her teens. Of course, she knew she'd been adopted, and there was a chance her family had been fishermen, or something like that. But Monica imagined the familiarity had something to do with the house itself, the garden and water, all giving her the strange impression of a life previously lived.

Perhaps it was simply the first time she felt like she'd finally found home.

Upon finishing undergraduate school, Monica's excellent grades had offered her entrance into every law school in the U.S. and beyond, but she'd decided only to apply to schools on the east coast. She wanted to get as far away from Los Angeles as she could, and even visited New York, but the endless black dresses and shoes, coats and scarves, all banishing the sunlight amidst the mountains they called sky scrapers…Well, the place just wasn't in her blood.

Instead she went to Maryland, but decided that while the summers were hot, the winters were much too cold. She had never known cold, and didn't want to, so she focused her attention further south. Virginia Beach? It was still too cold, and the same for the Carolinas. She was looking at brochures for schools in Spain when she got a call from Shelly.

Her friend was so excited she could hardly talk, telling Monica that she'd met a guy.

"Well, not *a* guy…*the* guy! We're going to get married!"

After several hours on the phone, Monica knew everything there was to know about Pepe Torentez, a cop. The spontaneity of it all was shocking enough, but Shelly marrying *a cop?* That left her speechless.

"My best friend is 'Pepper' and my husband, 'Pepe'! How cute is that?"

"I hate being called that," she grumbled, but somewhat relieved to hear that the Shelly she knew had returned once more.

# The Lost Dog

Monica cancelled her flight to Spain to travel home and share in the excitement. She became a regular third wheel on several of Pepe and Shelly's dates, and took a great liking to Pepe right away. He loved to talk about the crazy people he encountered every day and Monica and Shelly found his escapades endlessly exciting.

Alone, the two girls discussed the dangers of marrying a detective. Monica would try to steer Shelly away from her negative thoughts, even though she couldn't help feeling her fears were somewhat justified.

"You never know what will happen, in any job. Just take advantage of every single moment. Love him while you have him, for however long that may be."

And, Shelly did just that, even when her parents' protested at her choice of partner and refused to pay for the wedding. Shelly asked Monica if she would help, and since they no longer needed to make the Weisers happy, Shelly and Pepe chose to get married in Pepe's hometown of Miami, Florida.

Monica had no way of knowing that being Shelly's bridesmaid would change her life. Nor that Pepe's best man was a fellow police officer in Miami, with eyes so blue you could lose yourself in them, looking for the clouds.

From the moment she exited the plane, Monica felt a certain connection to the place. Walking outside from baggage claim, she realized it was the humidity, as it wrapped around her and moistened her skin, she couldn't help feeling comforted by something others generally found unpleasant.

Monica had a big 'to do' list when she stepped out of the Miami cab.

Within an hour of being embraced by its heat, its sun and its smiling people, Monica knew where she would be going to study, and best of all she'd be living near her best friend. She would have to enroll at the best law school there, and find an apartment near Pepe and Shelly, but first she had to finish the thousand and one responsibilities that were part and parcel of being Shelly's head bridesmaid.

On the wedding day she found herself escorted down the aisle by Pepe's best man, who'd shown up five minutes before the ceremony, minus his jacket, and gorgeous enough to steal the breath from her chest. Monica added one more thing to her list of attractions in Miami: Jeremy Harlan.

# CHAPTER FIFTEEN

Jeremy lay sprawled across the bed, morning sun streaming through the window. He hadn't slept well, finally falling into a fitful rest that was riddled with weird dreams. At that moment, he was dreaming he was back in high school, hiding behind the trophy case outside the principal's office. He'd been trying to pick the lock when an alarm had sounded, sending him for cover behind the large timber cabinet. There, he waited.

The alarm continued blaring on and off, on then off again, repeating over and over.

"Crap!"

He let out a deep breath and gathered his thoughts. It wasn't an alarm, just the bell signaling the start of class. Still, Jeremy felt comfortable where he was, even if his hiding place was claustrophobic.

After a brief pause the alarm sounded again, only this time it seemed louder. *That was a quick fourth period,* he thought. The bell was so loud it seemed to be wedged inside the cabinet--next to his head--and he stuck his arm into the cavity to find it, only to hit something cold and hard. For a moment he thought maybe Coach Dingman was lurking in the shadows, and had whacked his knuckles with a small, sharp object, likely his silver-plated whistle.

But the bell continued and finally Jeremy's brain woke up enough to order one eye open and survey the situation. The first thing he saw was his arm, sprawled over the clock radio next to a toppled aspirin bottle, and a photo of Jeremy and Monica kissing at *Arlos.*

Jeremy hit the clock once more, convinced that the damn thing was possessed, only to realize the persistent ringing wasn't coming from it anyway.

Next to his Glock nine-millimeter was his phone, buzzing angrily.

Picking it up and swiping the screen, Jeremy laid back on the pillows and looked at the ceiling for further evidence that he had in fact woken up, and that some new alarm wasn't going to start somewhere, the nightmare continuing.

"Detective Harlan."

It was Pepe, and as his friend asked him how he was, Jeremy could detect the faint whiff of judgment beneath his concern. They had always worked the same cases and worked pretty much the same hours. But lately Jeremy had been working later and sleeping in, and Pepe preferred being across every inch of his life.

"Out late again, huh?"

Pepe's tone was friendly, but he'd been dropping enough hints lately for Jeremy to know he was trying to find out if he had something on the side, like a woman. Every cop had plenty of opportunities to cheat; it was true what they said about women loving a man in uniform. And Jeremy…well, Pepe often said he'd never seen a cop attract more attention than Detective Harlan. But opportunity was only one part of a crime, and Jeremy lacked a motive. Anyone with eyes could see his wife was more than most men could ever dream of, let alone come home to every night.

Jeremy suppressed his annoyance and kept his tone light.

"Shelly been putting ideas in your head, partner?"

Pepe hated it when Jeremy suggested that his wife influenced him in any way, but she did, and was likely prodding him for information. Out to dinner recently, Monica had mentioned his late nights, and Shelly's brows had shot up so fast he thought they might fly right off her head.

"No," he said gruffly. "I just know that where there's a stink, it ain't too hard to find the shit."

If one thing was for sure his partner knew him better than anyone, perhaps even Monica. And for the first time in their long friendship, Jeremy didn't have a smart ass response.

# CHAPTER SIXTEEN

The rustling sounds coming from Jeremy's line had matched that of a fumbling hand. When his partner finally answered with, "Detective Harlan," it had sounded a little overdone--as if to say, "*I'm not sleeping!*"

But whatever the guy's problems were, he didn't want to talk about them, and Pepe knew better than to push. Besides, some bad things were going down in town.

He heard Jeremy sigh. "Another one?"

Pepe confirmed it, and went on to explain some of the details surrounding the latest body. It was starting to look like they had a serial killer on their hands.

"When can you get here?"

"I'm on my way."

This was the third time Pepe had woken Jeremy up with such news. The first time a woman had been killed, Jeremy and Pepe hadn't caught the case. Instead, it had been assigned to Schmidt and Roddy.

The victim was in her mid-thirties, and married. From all indications it had been a random homicide, but the detectives didn't want to rule anything out. Turned out she had a boyfriend, who looked like a good lead, but then his alibi checked out. Besides, their relationship had been pretty physical, and didn't seem to have the emotional makings for a crime of passion.

Then there was the husband, but he didn't know his wife was unfaithful until she'd turned up dead, and when he did find out, he went so mental that it didn't seem an act. He too had a watertight alibi. There were no enemies to be found, and no problems at work as the woman was a stay-at-home wife.

She'd been found outside the city between Ft. Lauderdale and Miami, at a rest area just off the highway. Her car was at the scene, and it was clear that she'd been strangled with a rope-like material. Her wallet was found close to her body, a fifty dollar bill and photo of her husband holding their Pug dog, still inside.

Schmidt and Roddy were totally lost. Word got around the precinct and everyone was aware of the case, but no closer to a lead.

Roddy's theory was that it was just someone in the wrong place at the wrong time. He figured that whoever committed the murder was long gone and way up north somewhere. And that theory seemed to work fine for Schmidt, who was four months from retirement. Chances were some sicko had waved her car down, and she'd been nice--or stupid--enough to stop.

Then, another murder had occurred, and another. All three taking place within two months, and all of them women around the same age, strangled, with minimal suspects or leads.

It had only been a matter of time before the case got thrown over to Pepe and Jeremy, and that day had finally come. This would be their first chance to see a fresh crime scene, instead of a series of 8x10 photos and a body in the morgue.

Together, Pepe and Jeremy had a track record of thirty-three homicide cases over thirteen years, and every case closed with a conviction. They were the best.

Jeremy lay staring at the ceiling fan, wondering what he was going to do. He had to come up with something, some sort of lead…something to turn the investigation in a new direction. This was one time Jeremy knew he needed to be smarter than everyone else, even his best friend and partner, Detective Pepe Torentez.

His mind raced backwards and forwards.

He could hear Monica moving around the kitchen, the smell of freshly made coffee making him feel slightly ill. Bleary eyed, he stumbled into the bathroom and stopped at the mirror.

The man looking back at him was like someone he'd never seen before, his features completely foreign. Then again, they were entirely too familiar.

He was the age his father had been when he was a young boy, and he almost expected the figure in the glass to order him to do a salute and give an 'oorah'.

He turned to the shower and twisted the faucet until the water was scorching. Stepping underneath, he scrubbed at his skin, readying himself for the dirt and grime of the city he was about to immerse himself in. He spent each and every day surrounded by street girls, drugs and money. And lately, a lot of corpses.

Jeremy would tell Pepe, *"If you want to catch a murderer, you gotta think like one."*

*"No shit amigo, that's Po-Po: 101."*

He'd said the next line so many times, it made Pepe roll his eyes.

*"Yeah, but what they don't teach you is that to think like a murderer…"* His friend slapped his hand on his shoulder as they said in unison, *"You gotta kill someone!"*

# CHAPTER SEVENTEEN

No homicide detective relished investigating a murder, but the sad reality was that if they didn't happen, they'd be out of a job.

Pepe was waiting for Jeremy in the station parking lot, leaning against the passenger door of their Ford Taurus. Like most of the cars in the lot it looked plain; no sense in having hubcaps when they were destined to become trophies for punk kids and local gangs.

Pepe didn't mind the car, but he did mind driving, so Jeremy begrudgingly played chauffeur each day. At six-foot-four, he cussed the department for selecting mid-sized automobiles.

With coffee between his legs and knees high enough to steer, Jeremy somehow managed to peel a banana as he drove them towards the crime scene. But Pepe wasn't focused on his reckless driving, rather he was wondering where his partner had been the night before.

Jeremy reached for the radio and informed dispatch they were *10-9*. He placed it back in the clip and finished eating the banana, before tossing the peel into the foot-well at Pepe's shoes.

Pepe didn't flinch, his loafer scooting the fresh peel towards the small pile of black peels that neither of them felt inclined to remove.

"It's about time we got the call for this one, huh?"

Jeremy chewed the banana, eyes scanning the street as he retained his thoughtful silence. Persistent, Pepe tried another tack.

"You stay out late again last night?"

Before he could reply Jeremy slammed on the brakes, the car squealing sideways across the street. Along with the peels and half of Jeremy's coffee,

Pepe was thrown hard against the passenger door. He stared at the traffic screeching to a stop around them.

"Damn it, Jeremy!"

He watched as his partner turned the car in an easy arc that sent them heading back in the opposite direction.

"You didn't see that?"

Pepe looked at him in confusion. Jeremy sped up the street only to slam on the brakes a second time, coming to a stop a few doors down from an empty car lot.

"See what?"

"Pepe, today is the day the narc boys are running their undercover sting behind Milbies."

Pepe was processing the words. He knew the case well; two officers had been working it for over fifteen months undercover.

"So?"

Jeremy sat, glaring through the windscreen with an intensity Pepe had only seen a couple of times prior. Once, when he'd shot a meth dealer straight through the head, and a second time, when he'd stood at the altar and watched Monica walking down the aisle.

"Call for back up Pepe, get everybody over here right now."

Once Pepe had made the call, Jeremy nodded towards a commercial dumpster that was partially hidden from the main road by a tall brick wall.

"All down the street dumpsters are over flowing with trash, the day before pickup," Jeremy murmured. "But not that one."

It was true. The dumpster behind the bar was neatly closed, but there was a hell of a lot of trash around its base. Standing about ten meters away was a weedy guy in a white singlet and jeans, clearly not carrying any weapons.

"Someone's waiting in that dumpster," Jeremy said, his eyes boring two holes through it.

The undercover officers parked at the rear of the bar, spotting their contact standing near a large dumpster.

As they exited the vehicle, the younger of the two narrowed his eyes at the trash piled against the side of the bin.

"Hey, Tony take a—"

Before the words had escaped him, the dumpster lid flew open to reveal four men brandishing assault rifles. The shortest of the four wore a white, sleeveless shirt that showed off the tattoos along his arms.

"You gonna die today, bros."

With a nimble hop the gang leader was out of the bin and walking across the concrete, gun held firmly in his hands.

"Shoulda never stepped out of that car."

He forced the officer to get down on his knees, his fingers locked and hands behind his head. The cop could feel the handle of his Glock pressed against the small of his back, so close, and yet too far to reach in time. The drug lord started to lift his gun, and the sound came only a split second before a fine mist covered the officer's face.

It was blood.

He'd always thought getting shot would hurt, but as the bang went off he felt no pain. In fact he felt nothing at all.

The thug fell to his knees beside him, clutching his chest as blood ran from between his fingers. It made no sense, they had no back up. The officer looked up, wondering if one of the gang's men had hit their leader by mistake, only to watch the remaining thugs collapse one by one, straight into the dumpster they were standing in. Headshots, all three of them, and their blood ran thick down the open lid behind them.

Their contact, a weasel called "Marco", was cowering on the ground, hands over the back of his head.

"I'm not armed!" he screamed.

The officers spun towards the source of the shots and saw Detective Harlan sauntering towards them with gun drawn, Detective Torentez running around the side of the building.

Harlan's face was set, hard as stone. "Y'all okay?"

The young cop tried to spit the man's blood out of his mouth, as his partner stood silently beside him, apparently in shock.

"Well go on…one of y'all call it in. Or did you do it already?"

Harlan lifted himself up the side of the bin and peered into its depths, while Torentez cuffed Marco, pulling the man's arms behind his back. Once he was secured, he turned to his partner, face pale beneath his tan.

"You crazy man?"

Harlan laughed.

"You could have waited for me. You got a death wish or something?"

Harlan slapped his hand on Torentez's shoulder. "There was no time, partner. You move too slow."

Seconds later sirens could be heard in the distance, and chopper blades thumped through the skies above them.

The young cop walked over to the detective. "Ah, Detective Harlan?"

Two cool blue eyes sliced straight through his. "Yeah?"

"I just want to say...thank you. I mean..." he stammered, trying to find words that felt adequate. Harlan waved him away.

"All in a day's work man."

Numerous squad cars surrounded them, along with firefighters, fire engines, ambulances, paramedics, the coroner...and finally the chief of police. The chief rarely came to a crime scene, but he knew his way around one. He was a wise man, and the whole city called him 'Cosby' or 'The Cos'. It wasn't his name, but he answered to it. His real name was Reginald Dorsey, but he reminded everyone of Bill Cosby, which added a great deal to his popularity.

The young officer felt a wave of nausea as the chief stared him down.

"Son, this could have been bad... real bad."

He loosened his steely stare and pointed his eyes toward Harlan.

"As for you...Are you crazy, Detective?"

"Why the hell is everybody asking me that?"

"'Cause you're a freak Harlan, a damn good cop, but a freak." The two dark eyes scanned the scene. "I mean, we got four guys, four guns, three of them Uzis, and one with a nine-mil." He paused then continued, louder. "Did they get off a single round?"

The young cop shook his head.

"Did you even draw your gun, son?"

He looked at his boots. "I couldn't reach it in time, Chief. It all happened so fast."

"We had two narc guys involved in the sting, and neither of you got off a single shot?" His voice was rising. "But there were four shots fired? And four kills?"

When the young cop spoke, the shame in his voice had been replaced by awe. "He was just driving by, sir. It's a miracle."

Cos gave a deep rumbling laugh, eyes latched on Harlan's back as the six-foot cop walked away with the coroner.

"Thank God he is on our side boy, or you'd be cold by now."

# CHAPTER EIGHTEEN

After reading Monica's text, Shelly placed her phone on the table and continued her discussion with the restaurant owner, Arlo. Monica would arrive any moment, and Shelly had turned up early to go through some of the arrangements Jeremy had asked her to manage. The surprise party was set for a few weeks, and Jeremy had delegated the decorations, menu, and wine to her. She loved being involved, and couldn't wait to see Monica's face at the big reveal.

"She will be here any minute, so don't say a word, Arlo."

"About what?"

They spun around and found the beautiful brunette staring at them curiously. Arlo's face turned a deep purple.

"Why, nothing bad, I promi-"

Shelly put her hand on his arm, trying to calm him before he had a heart attack.

"I was just telling Arlo I wanted to pay the bill this evening, Honky, but now you've gone and wrecked it."

Monica laughed; she always found Shelly's nickname hilarious, even after all these years. Off the hook, Arlo scuttled behind the bar and the two women took a table out on the patio. As they waited for their host to return with the usual steaming cups of coffee, Shelly could see that something was troubling her friend. She didn't need to be a detective to know that only man trouble could cause a frown like that.

Shelly had always pressed Monica to do more with her life, to apply herself, her smarts and her education. She couldn't help but feel frustrated that her friend spent each and every day penned up in a house cutting flowers, and waiting for her husband to come home. She wanted Monica to put to use the things she had worked so hard for, but they'd had the conversation countless times before, and it always went down the same dead end road...her dedication to Jeremy.

As if psychic, Monica started to say something about her husband working a lot of late nights. This time, Shelly was having none of it. If Monica knew her real thoughts about his actions lately...well, it was probably best to avoid the topic altogether.

Instead she focused on inspiring her friend. "You are so freaking smart, girl. Why don't you put that head of yours towards something more than worrying where Jeremy is at night?"

Monica looked up at her sharply, but Shelly ignored it, pretending to study the menu. "I only mean, of course you're going to worry because you've got little more than a dog and a garden to distract you. But don't you want more than that? More out of life?"

She waved her hand at Monica's objection before it could leave her lips.

"Monica, you have a law degree. You could be helping people!"

This gave her beautiful friend pause. Shelly knew that fame and fortune held no sway over Monica, but helping people...That always stopped her in her tracks. This time however, Monica looked pissed.

"Don't you think I get that, Shelly? Of course I want to help people. After all, I was pulled from the gutter myself, right?"

"You know I don't mean tha—"

"I've been given everything, right? So it's time to give back?"

Shelly was shocked to see the glimmer of tears in her friends eyes.

"Your parents were assholes, babe. I know that. You don't owe anyone anything." She slipped her hand across the table and grasped Monica's fine fingers within her own. "You only owe yourself. No one else."

The large brown eyes looked up, dark lashes wet with tears.

"Jeremy's been away so much lately, and I just feel so useless sitting there..."

"So don't sit there!" She gave her fingers an extra squeeze for emphasis. "I know you love that man, but you were born to do more than wait at home while he's off pursuing his dreams. You've got skills, girl. And an education most people would kill for…never mind the best pair of legs in town. You've gotta work it, or you'll go crazy."

Monica nodded, a small smile breaking through her sadness. "Yes," she whispered. "You're right."

# CHAPTER NINETEEN

Jeremy and Pepe had no time to fill out a police report on the shooting, and Cosby said not to worry about it. They were needed at their original destination, the homicide scene of the third victim. It was looking like they might have a serial killer on their hands, and so the psyche exams—mandatory for every cop who shot someone—were put on hold as well.

There was no music in the car as they headed toward the homicide scene. The only sound was from the two walkie-talkie units each detective had laid down near the center console.

Pepe, behind the wheel for once, stared straight ahead and kept silent. He did his best to watch his partner out of the corner of his eye. The guy had just killed four men, and yet he was...calm. Peaceful, almost. Occasionally he grabbed at his t-shirt collar, pulled it over his nose and wiped away at a bead of sweat, but other than that, nothing.

They'd been driving about ten minutes when Jeremy reached out and opened the glove box. He dug around in it for a few seconds, and was evidently unsuccessful in his search. Slamming it shut, he then flipped the sun visor down, only to be disappointed with that search as well. He snapped it back into place.

The thick silence was broken by the radios crackling to life.

*"Ten-two Charlie, ten-two Charlie. Ten-fifty-four Abbot and Wilkes, ten-fifty-four."*

*"Caller identifies..."*

They both reached to adjust the volumes, Pepe saying, "I'll turn mine down, leave yours up."

"I'm turning mine down," Jeremy snapped. "I don't care what you do with yours."

Pepe tried his best smile. "Well, one of us has to have it turned up, *vato*." Then he remembered that Jeremy had just shot and killed three four men. "Sorry Jay, I ain't thinking. I know you just popped four *caballeros*."

There was silence in the car, Jeremy seeming to ignore him. A moment later he was unbuckling his seatbelt to twist and look under his feet. For a man his size, it felt like the whole car moved with each new exertion.

"Dude, what are you looking for?"

"I don't mind getting blood on my hands, then getting sent off to another job, but I do mind going without my piece." He was feeling underneath the seat again, and Pepe finally understood. Jeremy was unarmed, his own gun taken by the chief as part of the investigation that would now surround the death of the gangsters.

"Jay, quit looking around for another gun, bro. I don't have a throw-away…at least not in here."

Jeremy was now checking underneath Pepe's seat. Pepe gripped the steering wheel a little tighter.

"Man, quit feeling up underneath me. I told you I don't have another piece on me."

The car slowed as they reached the curb beside a large public park. Nearby they could see the taped off barrier. Pepe shut the engine off as Jeremy began to remove his tie, handing it to Pepe.

"What the hell are you doing?"

"Well, I'm not trying to find another gun, dumbass—I got one strapped to my right ankle. I was trying to find a napkin."

"*Una sevilleta?*"

"And since you don't have one, my tie will do the job."

Jeremy reached out and turned the rearview mirror so that Pepe could see his face. A smear of blood ran across his hairline, where he'd swiped at the sweat. Pepe gladly took the tie from Jeremy and began to wipe at the mark.

"Ugh, I must have touched one of them without thinking. Sorry man, to make you look at the antifreeze leaking from those dudes. *Lo siento amigo*." He finished cleaning up and threw Jeremy's tie to the floor, amidst the spilt coffee and banana peels.

"I ain't worried about seeing blood Pep, I just don't want you contaminating this crime scene with your ugly grill." Pepe punched him and he laughed. "That's how O.J. got off, you know?"

Pepe opened his door smiling, pleased to see his partner in good spirits. They grabbed their radios, turned their volumes up slightly and got out of the car. He ducked underneath the yellow tape as Jeremy raised it.

"If the glove don't fit, you gotta acquit!" Pepe said, smirking.

They both laughed, popping on their rubber gloves. He knew that this was how Jeremy dealt with pain. His laughter was his own form of release, without emotional indulgences he couldn't allow.

The world was crazy. Sometimes, you're sanity depended on getting a little crazy too.

# CHAPTER TWENTY

As soon as they passed beneath the yellow tape they fell silent. He knew Pepe would go straight to the victim, but Jeremy kept his back to them, focused instead on the outside perimeter.

The long, yellow ribbons had always irritated Jeremy.

He had nothing against the color, but he did resent the need for its use in the first place. No one seemed to have respect for the police and their work, and he thought people were sick in the way they craved gore and violence. Whole mobs would surround crime scenes, video cameras and phones held above heads as they tried to get a glimpse of something gruesome to share on social media. They had no respect for the person who'd just lost their life and become another headline.

So the police put up their tape; another procedure. Jeremy, not being a fan of procedure, still understood the need for this one. But he thought it made a detective lazy, and sometimes hurt more than it helped.

He had worked with many a detective who would approach a crime scene and assume that they were only to investigate inside that yellow square. Many, many things were missed because they lay just beyond the yellow threshold. So, Jeremy always began his investigations like a cow put out to pasture. He would walk the perimeter fence slowly, as if looking for an exit, a gap in the posts or a way to get out...one little flaw that could make all the difference it the world. He'd solved many cases outside the yellow tape.

Jeremy never paid much attention to the obvious. He knew by now that Pepe would already have established the time of death from the coroner, and he knew his partner would be studying the body, personal belongings, position, defensive wounds and such. He would also know almost immediately if the body had been dumped, or if they were at the actual scene of the crime.

As his partner worked, Jeremy allowed himself to slip into the mentality of a murderer. A public restroom stood just outside the yellow tape, about sixty feet to the southeast behind a clump of trees. Someone might have used it to hide in, or clean up…but by now the uniforms had most likely been in there and trampled the place.

The park was full of buttonwood trees in full bloom, bees humming above their heads. For a brief moment he allowed himself to think about his beautiful wife. She loved that kind of stuff. He caught himself thinking of her smile, the delicious curve of her hip, when there was a young woman lying dead, only a few feet away.

Jeremy suppressed the thoughts of Monica and focused once more on the scene around him. To the north were silvery palm trees, tall and straight and surrounded by blue-eyed grass.

How did he know the names of these things? Monica. Married to woman who talked to plants and flowers more than her own husband, he was bound to learn something. And he knew the name of blue-eyed grass mainly because it wasn't a grass at all. He'd found that out the hard way.

The first time he'd heard Monica mention the name he'd perked up, thinking he could finally help her out with something. She had obviously confused the black-eyed Susie flower with the blue grass of Kentucky. And he'd told her so, laughing at her mistake. He'd laughed and laughed, until he noticed her silence.

"Honey, are you done?"

Jeremy was still chuckling, albeit a little nervously.

Monica went into professor mode.

"First off, *Detective* Harlan, please seat yourself at the computer where, if it pleases the court, I will ask you to Google 'blue-eyed grass.'"

Jeremy was quick to sit down and prove her wrong, but he should have known better.

# The Lost Dog

"While you are discovering your own ignorance, it's my sad responsibility to also inform you, that there is no such thing as a 'black-eyed Susie.' The correct terminology would be a 'black-eyed Susan.'"

Jeremy stopped laughing when the webpage loaded, and he was faced with endless pictures of star shaped flowers. They weren't even blue, but purple, and he snorted at the screen, as if to say the whole thing was ridiculous.

"Susie, Susan, what's the difference? They'd come running if you called either name.'"

"They are flowers, Your Honor, incapable of running."

For a moment as he cast his eyes through the trees he could almost smell the scent of her on the breeze...God, he loved her.

More than life itself.

# CHAPTER TWENTY-ONE

Pepe was wrapping up his conversation with the coroner, who had established the time of death to be around 11:30P.M. the night prior. They both agreed the murder had likely happened at the scene, and that the woman had been strangled in the same manner as the other victims. There were no signs of any struggle, which was also consistent. But the forensic investigators were puzzled as to what these women had been strangled with.

Dr. Matt Credo was the chief medical examiner for Miami Dade County, and popped his rubber gloves off as he spoke with Pepe.

"I wish I could tell you something more. Other than the strangulation, the only thing consistent about these murders is the amount of force. They were likely strangled by the same person, the depth of the ligature marks is almost identical. What's strange though is that the perp is not trying to decapitate them. From what I can gather, they've been choked gently, if that makes any sense."

"So were the strangulations intentional? I mean, was the perp trying to kill them?"

"Hell, yeah." The older man looked down at the crumpled body. "And the person responsible was big."

"Why do you say that, if the killings were 'soft'?"

"To hold the victim and keep them from thrashing about would take size and strength. This was a big guy, most likely." He looked up and nodded towards Jeremy. "I'd say Harlan's size."

As if hearing his name, Jeremy walked back up to them.

"Hold up gentlemen," Credo called out to the coroner boys, who'd begun to zip up the bag.

He gestured for them to squat beside him, and nodded for one of his assistants to turn the face of the victim. Pepe's heart clenched as he saw how young and beautiful she was. It shouldn't have made a difference, but it did.

The assistant turned the chin of the victim and Pepe noticed that Jeremy turned away. It was unusual for him to be squeamish, but the guy had had a tough day.

Credo continued. "You can see this is certainly similar to our other victims, but when I compared this to photos from the other murders, I noticed that the fiber content and width of the implement used varies for each one."

"Are you sure about that?" Pepe asked.

Jeremy turned to him and scowled. "Dammit, Pepe, why the hell would he tell you if he wasn't sure?" Standing up he brushed his hands against his trousers. "Zip her up and get her out of here."

As Jeremy stomped off, Pepe looked at Credo. The man said nothing, but his raised brows spoke volumes.

"He can yell at me if he likes," Pepe said defensively. "My firstborn will carry his name regardless. If it's a girl she'll be the only Jeremy in a dress."

Credo smiled and nodded, but his eyes remained cool.

"Jay's a hero," Pepe continued. "He saved lives today, friend. And don't you forget it."

# CHAPTER TWENTY-TWO

Like many young men who had the fortune—or despair—to be around Monica, Arlo's son Dominic had a crush that made Romeo Montagues' pale in comparison.

But his crush was different to the others, or so he believed. By never allowing Monica to know he was crazy about her, Dominic was sure it would somehow make him special, and this in turn would force her to fall for him. So for this reason he never spoke of his feelings for her. Well, that and the threat of Jeremy Harlan kicking his ass.

Still, a young man had to dream.

Standing by their table, he held out a handkerchief to Monica as he spotted a tear at the corner of her eye. She had reached for her sunglasses, but he'd made it to her side before she could put them on.

She smiled at him, taking the cloth from his fingers. As she did so, Dominic could not help but notice her wedding band. His stomach twisted at the sight. It was a tragedy of epic proportions that she was married, but the ring itself was so...*nothing!* A plain, simple wedding band, for a woman worth a trillion diamonds.

*If she were mine, I'd buy her the biggest diamond in all of South Beach.* He could barely afford the payments on his 1989 Firebird, but that didn't matter. He would find a way, beg, borrow and steal if he had to. Dominic's eyes traveled from her hands to her lips, and fixed there, refusing to move on. Then his name started sinking in.

*Dominic...Dominic...*

"Dominic?"

He snapped back into reality when his father kicked his shoe.

"Dominic, the ladies are trying to have a conversation. Why don't you do your job, and get them a fresh round of coffees?"

Arlo apologized to the women, and, seeing the glisten in Monica's eyes, asked if the news had shocked her badly.

"What news?" The question didn't come from Monica, but Shelly.

"Oh my God, *la mia bellezza è*, Arlo is so sorry." His father looked at them in surprise, and started to ramble something about bodies and shootings.

Shelly sprung up from the table, phone in hand, as Monica looked off into the distance, her beautiful eyes glazed over. Arlo hovered above her, doing his best to undo the damage by repeating again and again they were fine, heroes even. Finally, he threw his hands in the air and pointed to the television screen in the corner.

"Haven't you been watching?"

Monica, wiping away more tears managed to say, "What happened?"

As Arlo held her in his arms, Dominic stood in the corner wishing he'd thought of it himself. In truth, he'd missed the news story as well.

"Dominic, coffee!" his father hissed.

Shelly walked back and slammed her phone on the table. "Neither of them are answering. What the hell happened, Arlo?"

"Her husband shoots the bad guys," he pointed at Monica. Cocking his finger he added, "Four men, bang, bang, BANG!" he said, and the women jumped.

Dominic placed the coffees at their table and leant down to hug Monica. Before he'd even wrapped his arms around her his father was wrenching him up by the collar.

"Let us make you Pastitsio, ladies! Hmm?"

He looked at Dominic, who was still holding onto Monica's shoulder with a death grip. He liked the feel of her neck beneath his fingers, the sense of ownership inherent in the stance. Arlo, staring a hole through his son, came as close as possible to yelling, while managing to maintain his smile.

"Dominic, let go of this one and go to the oven. The ladies are worried for their *husbands*."

69

He clapped his hands and motioned toward the kitchen, Dominic managing to sneak a kiss on Monica's forehead.

"I will get you our best wine," said Arlo. "You sit, you talk, be thankful today; your mens are heroes!" he beamed, waddling behind the bar. Head drooped, Dominic followed.

# CHAPTER TWENTY-THREE

Monica and Shelly sat for a while and tried to breathe, still too shocked to feel the full benefit of their relief. The silence lasted for a moment, and then, like a pair of simmering volcanoes they erupted with questions about what had just taken place.

The wine flowed freely—Arlo trying to make up for his earlier lapse—and when the story came back on the TV he called them over to the bar. They stood resting their arms on the stool backs, eyes set on the mounted screen and wine glasses firmly clutched in hand.

It was a brief story, not much video in the way of their two husbands, though they did show them at the crime scene talking to Cos. Jeremy had his face tipped down and was nodding slowly, Pepe staring at his friend with an expression of disbelief.

The walk back to their table was a touch wobbly, and when Shelly put her glass down Monica asked for another bottle. Her friend raised a brow, but smiled. After all, death had brushed past both their families that day.

They were happy their husbands would be coming home, but it was also a reminder that one day they might not. No wife ever really believed it would happen, but they had both consoled young, distraught women who'd been proven wrong.

At the table they waited for their second bottle of Arlo's best Italian wine, made from the finest sangiovese grapes. Monica looked at the jewel red liquid at the bottom of her glass, and shivered at its similarity to blood. She rolled it around slowly, a single thick drop, not so different to what her husband had likely been covered in only an hour ago. Jeremy had singlehandedly killed four men…

As the wine continued its lazy loop, Monica started talking about the fact she didn't know her husband like she should, and that if he were to die, she would have so many unanswered questions. It seemed inconceivable to her that he should have to carry the weight of so much risk on his own; if anything were to happen, she would feel that she had let him down. Monica was vaguely aware of her hands waving around as her words became more frustrated. After all, she was smart, intelligent, and a good wife. She had a lot to offer a homicide detective, particularly one with a taste for danger. Her husband needed support, information and protection.

When Shelly put one hand atop hers, and pried the empty wine glass from her fingers, Monica realized she'd grown breathless. How much had she said? "I want to help him, Shelly," she finished lamely.

Shelly nodded, settling back into her seat.

"Shell, I have been offered jobs from prosecutors, district attorneys and law firms all over the country. Why not get involved in my own husband's life? I want to get to know him." She slapped her palm down on the table. "I *need* to know him."

"Go Honky. I love the fire, let it burn baby."

Dominic arrived with a fresh bottle and the two friends smiled across the table as he refilled their glasses. Once he'd scuttled off Shelly raised it and clinked it against Monica's.

"To all the wives of our men."

They nodded solemnly and took a sip, but a moment later Monica had lifted her glass once more.

"I herby pledge, to my best friend in the entire world…" She lowered her voice and peeked over the glass, "Shelly, you know you are my best friend, right?" Shelly's face softened, but Monica didn't wait for an answer. "I hereby pledge that, having realized the fragile hand of the clock that we cannot control…I, Monica Harlan—" at this point she hiccupped, and Shelly giggled "—promise to love my husband with all my heart and soul."

# The Lost Dog

Then, almost like throwing a haymaker, Monica heaved her glass forward and *CLANK!* Both were surprised when the glasses didn't break, and Monica took it as a good omen. She had sealed the deal.

"I will start my pledge tonight …after I finish the other bottle."

"What other bottle?"

"Any other bottle Shelly, any other bottle!"

# CHAPTER TWENTY-FOUR

The forensics office wasn't much like the set of one of those glitzy crime shows on TV. Instead of stainless steel there was Formica, and not a single dazzling LED to be seen; this room was illuminated by flickering fluorescents that made the place green. There wasn't even any fancy lab stuff, the technicians had to send out to get that done. And there certainly weren't halls full of young, attractive women in white coats and trendy glasses; in fact, there wasn't even a hall to begin with. Just 'Autopsy Al'—Alex Mendezio.

Al's office reminded Jeremy of the various barracks he and his father would visit when traveling on vacation to Camp *This* or Camp *That*.

John Harlan would say, "Boy, you know we're only sixty-two clicks from a United States Marine Corps camp?" Without fail, this statement was immediately followed by a ritual that made Jeremy's stomach clench.

"Can I get a *hoo-rah*?"

His dad would shout the words as if he were standing back in bootcamp, one big fist punching Jeremy's side. As a young boy without much meat on his bones, each knock hurt and his dad knew it, but the unwritten law persisted. Jeremy was never going to whimper.

Jeremy had learned very early that when his dad said, *"Can I get a hoo-rah?"* he had better give it back before the second punch landed. And the screaming part actually proved quite helpful; it took his mind off of the pain settling around his ribs.

After John had satisfied whatever it was inside him that craved this kind of interaction, he would say, *"Semper fi boy; always faithful."*

The older Jeremy got, the bigger and stronger he became, and he began to attract the attention of recruiters from every college in the nation. The more accomplishments the teen achieved on the football field, the more his father flaunted him all over the south, and especially at the Maine Corps camps.

He had been showcased at Camp Pendleton, Camp Lejeune, and Jeremy's favorite, the Marine Corps base at Quantico.

Jeremy liked visiting Quantico due to the air facility there, but it was this very interest that ensured he never got to go back. John Harlan would not stomach a son who fought from the seat of an aircraft.

Pepe stood by the door waiting for Al to finish talking into a tape recorder he held close to his lips. From a boom box in the corner played Dean Martin's, *"Baby it's Cold Outside."*

His partner looked at the victim on the table, and leaned in to Pepe's ear. "I'm gonna sit this one out, man," said Jeremy. "I ain't feeling too good. I'll be in the car."

Pepe watched Jeremy walk off, wondering if the shooting had affected the man more than he'd first guessed. But he hadn't just been acting strange for hours; he'd been acting strange for months. This was their first serial killer case, if it *was* a serial killer, and instead of bucking up, Jeremy seemed to want to sit the whole thing out. But this was a detective's dream job, and Jeremy was one of the most ambitious cops he'd ever met.

Dr. Mendezio clicked the small recorder and placed it back inside the front pocket of his lab coat.

"So, is it the same killer?"

Al, being the card he was, began singing and rewriting the lyrics to the Deano song still playing on the boom box. "I really can't say ... Why don't you go away?"

Pepe looked at him in confusion, until the doctor broke into a grin.

"Hi Pepe, how are you? Good to see you too!"

Pepe finally got the point.

"Sorry Doc, been a long day."

"Yeah, I heard. Thank God you guys are alright, yeah?"

He walked to the sink popping off his gloves, then reached over to turn down the music.

"Speaking of thanking God, I thought I caught a glimpse of our local hero. Where is Wild Bill Hickok?" He turned back around after washing his hands and grabbed a paper towel, wiping his hands and throwing it away. "He was in the other day without you, and now you're in today without him? Do I detect trouble in paradise?"

Pepe looked at Al. "He's out in the car…You know, the shooting and all. I think he might be shaken up."

"Jeremy? Shaken up?" The doctor laughed. "Who are you kidding? He's The Ice Man."

Pepe got out a pen and clicking the end—realized it was a pencil. No matter, it would do the trick. But he'd only gotten the time and date down before the lead snapped and bounced off the pad. He felt Al's eyes on him.

"You a bit shaken up too?"

"I'm good. Would you have a …"

Before he's finished the sentence Al was holding a pen out. He took it and thanked the man.

"So you were saying Jeremy was in here without me?"

"Yeah, actually now that I think about it, he's been in a couple of times."

Pepe masked his puzzlement as much as possible, hoping to maintain the impression he and his partner were on the same page. It was becoming clearer by the second that they weren't.

"Anyway, I'm pretty sure it's the same killer, Pepe. The amount of force used to constrict each vic's airflow has been the same. The strangulation patterns were identical, except for the width of the instrument used. So yes, I think you have a serial killer on your hands. None of these poor women had traces of any illegal substances in their blood after preliminary analysis; none were intoxicated. In fact, these are some the healthiest women I have ever seen on my table. Whoever did this had to get in close, almost intimately close."

Al walked around the table, brushing his gloved hands across the young woman's throat. "You see, usually when I see strangulation by a rope or cord, there are cuts above the ligature marks. Larger ones are often found on female victims." He paused. "Here let me show you."

Pepe tensed as Al went to stand behind him, pulling his belt free.

"You know I'm not into that fruity stuff, Doc."

The man laughed. "Now, if I were to place this belt around you from behind and begin to choke you with it…" He slipped the leather around Pepe's neck and squeezed—too tight for Pepe's comfort. His immediate reaction was to raise both hands and grab the belt, trying to pry it from his neck. The instant Pepe reacted this way, Al released him.

"See?"

"See what? That you were choking me!"

"Well, next time bring your hero partner and I'll strangle him."

"Yeah, and he'll shoot you in the head." Pepe raised two fingers, and cocked them back. "Boom."

It had sounded funny to Pepe as it left his mouth, but once airborne he wished he could take it back.

Al laughed, if a little forcefully, and continued on with his explanation. "When the belt was around you and you felt it tighten, your instinct was to pry it away." He lifted his hands to his own throat in demonstration. "When a person does that it causes the little cuts and scrapes we often see on victims who've been chocked."

Pepe nodded, and the doctor continued.

"This is the reason I see more secondary, self-inflicted wounds on females. Their nails being longer."

Pepe immediately walked to the body on the table and leaned over. At first sight he could not see any fingernail marks at all. Then, grabbing the autopsy light, he flicked it on and moved it down toward the neck of the corpse.

"Am I missing something here?"

"I am afraid not, Pepe. Look at her nails."

Pepe's eyes followed the arm down to her hands, picking one up and moving the light so he could see her nails. He rolled her fingers back and forth.

"Nothing, right?"

Al nodded.

"So somehow the vic was unable fight back…Have you ever seen anything like this before?"

Al lowered his chin to his chest. "No, but I am running through the database to see if there have been any other cases that are similar."

Once their briefing had been wrapped, the doc walked over and turned up the boom box, singing, "*When the moon hits your eye like a big pizza pie, that's amore.*"

Pepe shook his hand and thought Italian food sounded nice. He'd drive Jeremy to Arlo's, and from there they could call the girls and…shit! Had Jeremy called the girls? He pulled his phone out and saw missed calls from Shelly scattered throughout a dozen others from friends, family and the office. *Damn.*

Pepe ran down to the car and jumped into the driver's seat, started the engine, lowered the window and slammed the portable siren on the roof.

Jeremy sat up. "What the hell's going on?"

"*Vato*, how could you be so stupid?"

His partner's face flashed through a gallery of different emotions, confusion, surprise and…guilt?

"Stupid how?" he said quietly.

"The girls you *alcornoque*, did you call them?"

"No, why?"

"Hell, you saw the news cameras. This shit's gotta be all over TV, I've had about a dozen missed calls already, they'll be getting calls too."

Jeremy slumped his head back against the rest. "God, Monica's going to kill me."

He pulled out his phone and frowned.

"You got a dozen calls? I only got one."

Pepe snorted. "You're The Ice Man bro, I'm your only friend." He slipped through the traffic as it parted for all the noise and flashing lights. "Call the girls and make sure they hear the siren. We'll tell them we've been in pursuit of the same car all day."

Jeremy looked at him, then turned his gaze to the clock in the dash.

"For six hours? What, did we chase them all the way to Tampa and back?"

"Make up something! And tell them we'll meet them at Arlos. I want meatballs in my spaghetti, not ripped from my pants and served on a platter."

Jeremy laughed. "I'll do my best Pepe, but no promises."

# CHAPTER TWENTY-FIVE

The next morning Monica was slow getting up. Her eyes opened, and for a brief moment she wasn't quite sure where she was. She rolled onto her back with the back of her wrist resting on her forehead, and felt a wave of nausea as a snippet of memory from the night before began to surface.

Without thinking she reached out and placed her hand on Jeremy. She wasn't particular about where her hand might wind up, content just to touch him. She felt his body and gently rubbed her nails against him softly, then her fingers, and then the palm of her hand. His flesh was soft on the outside, but with a taught foundation underneath of muscle. Upon further investigation her fingers revealed there was no navel close by, so she began once again to focus on the inside of her palm for a final determination. And with a slight movement down a little valley into a fine fuzz of hair, she knew she had landed on Jeremy's thigh.

With her opposite hand on her unsettled stomach, Monica thought how easily her caress might lead to more, but at the same moment her body was pleading something different. She brought her hand up to her face and rubbed the outside of her eyelids with her fingers, still trying to wake up and un-scatter her thoughts.

*Let's see yesterday started with…* She rose up just a bit, enough to look over the edge of the bed and focus on the dark lump in the corner by the armoire.

*Grady.*

Lying back down, she hoped the dog hadn't heard her rustling between the sheets.

# The Lost Dog

Grady played this game every day. He would let her know he was ready to start the day by placing his slightly graying, very sophisticated snout on the side of her bed. In this position he retained a respectful silence, but would wag his tail so hard he almost knocked his back legs right out from under himself.

This was his, *Good morning, Momma... Please, please open the door so I can go pee* routine. For now however, he seemed content to sleep. She rolled over and put her arm around Jeremy, who was lying with his back toward her, and slid as close as she could get. Then a little closer still. She laid her arm over his shoulder and began to stroke his hair with her fingers, thinking about what he must have gone through the day before. Monica felt guilty about being too drunk to comfort him properly...or perhaps she had?

She let her hand slide down his arm, eventually resting on the back of his hand, then interlaced her slender fingers between his long ones, fastening her palm to the back of his hand. For some reason, this particular morning felt different. *He* felt different. Her mind couldn't shake that this was the hand that had killed four human beings. 'Bad guys' sure, but sons, brothers, people nonetheless. The thought of killing made her chest feel tight, and she couldn't imagine how anyone could carry that kind of pain.

Her mind continued burrowing its way through the ache of her hangover, and Jeremy's hand went from feeling like an extension of her own, to some strange, alien object pressed against her.

She loved him, and hated herself for thinking it, and yet the thought persisted. *I am holding the hand of a killer.*

# CHAPTER TWENTY-SIX

Monica was surprised by the tear that slid down her cheek. Two days in a row? Yesterday she had cried for the first time in over twenty years.

*What is happening to me?*

Then she remembered the toast, and the promise she had made. Pressed against the slow rise and fall of her husband's breathing, she began to feel a new sense of strength settle into her bones. Monica looked out the sliding glass door and listened to the ocean, closing her eyes and losing herself in its rhythm.

She concentrated on it, thinking of nothing else until the world melted away, and all she could hear was the soft pound of the waves, the push and pull of Jeremy's breathing.

And then, as if there were a loud whistle, the *what if* train left the station, and began speeding down the tracks of her mind. She wanted to derail it somehow, but it just seemed to pick up speed, going faster and faster—fueled by every unimaginable thing that might have happened to her husband. The train didn't have a final destination; she would have to jump off somehow to get on with her day, and her life.

So, she jumped.

Kissing Jeremy on the back of his neck, she felt him stir and wake, then turn in her arms. They spent the rest of that morning in a long communication, and not a word was wasted.

When they finally broke apart, Jeremy pulled back and looked at her with a smile playing across his lips.

# The Lost Dog

"Where did that come from?"

Hair tousled around her face and lips parted in expectation of their next kiss, Jeremy was much obliged to be loved in this way by his beautiful wife. He knew every day couldn't start the same way, but when they did it seemed to make him a better man, a better husband, a better detective, and a better... *Whoa.*

His next thought made him pause. He'd almost mused, *a better dad.*

Monica was watching him closely.

"What's wrong, baby?"

Jeremy lay silent for a moment, before drawing away from her to settle back into his pillow. "You'd make a good detective, you know that?" He sighed. "You don't miss a thing."

Monica sidled back up against him, tracing her fingers along the ridges of his chest. "It's funny you should say that," she said, continuing the slow movement up and down. "I was talking to Shelly..." Jeremy felt a ball of lead settle in his guts. This couldn't be good. "And baby, I realized that I don't really know you...as much as I want to."

The last few words almost squeaked out of her, and as much as he wanted to relieve her nervousness, he wasn't able to overcome the darkness that was shutting down his brain. Monica kept on.

"You keep so many things from me, and you know I don't need to know everything right? I mean who wants to know everything?" She patted him softly, and he realized he'd stopped breathing. "But, Jeremy, you're my husband!" She sighed, the words spilling out of her. "I want to know what goes on inside you...I love you, I love the man I married, and I am so dedicated to loving you in every possible way."

Monica sat up in the middle of the bed, completely naked, with her knees folded underneath her and her hands resting on the top of her knees.

*She is so freaking beautiful,* he thought, while simultaneously waiting for the axe to fall.

"Jeremy." Monica spoke with a great deal of determination. "I want to get a job."

She didn't give Jeremy a chance to say no, or a chance to say anything at all. "Either as a lawyer or..." She squirmed a bit in the middle of the bed,

83

positioning herself just right to say whatever was about to come. "Or a private detective working in the crime lab, or something…I want to do something!"

She stared intently at her husband, as he waited for the shock to subside long enough to string a sentence together. Deep down, he'd always known this day must come. She was too smart, beautiful—amazing, to spend her days pottering around a house. But selfishly, he'd wanted to keep her locked away from the rest of the world. *His*. It had been the perfect marriage for him, but not for Monica. And so, the day of reckoning had come.

His first reaction was, of course, to turn to the dog for an exit strategy. "Grady!" He sat up in bed and looked toward the furry lump with apparent concern. "Monica, we need to let Grady out."

Grady bounced to Monica's side of the bed and rested his snout on the white sheet, wagging his entire body.

"Did you walk Grady?"

"Of course."

Jeremy knew she was lying but could do nothing about it. Grady wasn't going to stop something that had been inevitable from the start. Jeremy was going to have to face the realization that things were going to be different.

While he kept thinking, Monica kept talking. He could hear what she was saying, but his mind was processing all the stuff he'd had to hide from her, past and present. The openness she craved would affect his secrets, things he couldn't bring himself to say aloud.

She might find out what he had been doing lately. And what would she do if she did? Could she still love him, if she knew?

# CHAPTER TWENTY-SEVEN

The next ten days together proved vastly different to the thousands Monica and Jeremy had shared thus far. Monica had made a tipsy—but determined—promise, and had every intention of sticking to it.

Mornings were spent on the same small chores and pleasures, only now breakfast was peppered with questions about his work. She would start in on him from the moment he was dressed, having enough self control to at least allow him the space he needed to wake up, go to the bathroom, take a shower, and stumble into his jeans. But the second his zip was up, it was on.

She had tried hard not to make Jeremy feel like he was suddenly on the wrong side of the interrogator's table, although she could tell she was close to doing just that. For the first few days he hadn't appeared to mind too much. But as a week rolled by, Jeremy's showers seemed to last longer, and the time he spent picking out something to wear went from ten minutes to thirty. She knew she was getting on his nerves and was smart enough not to bring about her own destruction, so she backed off a bit. This took a great deal of self-discipline, as in just ten days Monica had come to love her newfound focus. It had given her a feeling she hadn't experienced since going to the library in LA County to try and find out who her real parents were. Monica's whole life had been filled with mystery, and so her desire for truth and resolution burned brighter in her than some of the most seasoned detectives.

For several years that library had become a second home to Monica, as she combed through news articles, journals, blogs and books searching for any clue that might help her understand where she had come from, and *whom*. If she could find the answer to either of those questions, or via some miracle both, she was sure history would help her unlock her future and understand her path in life.

This new mystery felt no different, she only hoped the experience would be more productive. Her efforts in the library had led to nothing, but her work now might just help Pepe and Jeremy find a serial killer. Where once she'd searched for herself, now she sought to save the lives of others.

Shelly smiled at the screen of her phone; it had been close to a week since her best friend had called.

"Honkey, how are you?"

This was met with a loud sigh, exhaustion tinged with contentment. "It took fourteen hours, but I think I've done it," Monica said, before going on to explain that after strenuous harassment, she'd finally sat her husband down and demanded he let her help with his cases.

"He just froze, Shell. It was like I'd asked him to move to Alaska."

Shelly wanted to be supportive, but the truth was she didn't know what to think. Something in the pit of her stomach led her to believe it was a bad idea, that her friend might discover a side to her husband that was better left alone. Still, it was all Monica would talk about for the next two hours, until the phone pressed to Shelly's ear was burning hot.

"Finally he seemed to cave a bit, and suggested we test the waters…you know start slow." There was a short burst of delighted laughter. "I mean, that's pretty much a 'yes', right!"

"Wow," Shelly did little to mask her surprise, even as she glanced at the clock and saw her morning was slipping away.

"I know. He suggested I get together with someone down at the precinct from time to time. He thought I might assist with research, or deal with enquiries from the press."

"Jeremy really said that?"

This did not fit at all with the man she knew, who kept a strict division between his private and working lives.

"Yes! He said he would set me up with anyone I wished to work with." The line grew quiet as she paused. "Well, anyone but Pepe. Apparently he doesn't want his wife sharing his partner." Monica laughed. "I said to him that was fine. But that if I could work with anyone at the precinct, it would have to be him. Oh Shelly, it was so beautiful. I'm telling you, I had him, I had him right where I have always wanted him."

Shelly couldn't help smiling at the excitement in her voice; a sound she hadn't heard in years. Still, she found it hard to muster the words of support Monica was so clearly seeking. Was it jealousy? No, Shelly could care less about crime fighting with Pepe, it actually terrified her to see his shoulder holster and pistol on the coat rack at home. When they had babies, things were going to change.

"Come on, Shell, don't you remember the toast? I've been dying to challenge myself, and get to know Jeremy better. I am actually getting to do both!"

Shelly laughed at the *pop...pop...pop-pop* of Monica's victory bubbles at the end of the line. "Of course I'm happy for you honey," she said, ignoring the uneasiness in her stomach. "Just be careful, OK?"

For the first time in over an hour her friend was quiet. Then, "Why do you say that, Shell?"

"I don't know Monica. But promise me you will be?"

When Monica spoke again the excitement seemed to have left her, and Shelly felt a pang of guilt. "Sure," Monica said. "But really, you really have nothing to worry about."

Shelly was sure she was right, but she just couldn't shift that feeling.

# CHAPTER TWENTY-EIGHT

Jeremy felt caged.

And it wasn't due to his confinement inside the four small walls of his bathroom, but what was waiting outside.

He was a reasonable man, and could understand his wife wanting to work, get out of the house and stretch her wings. But what made him feel trapped was her constant questioning. The mornings were spent in interrogation, then throughout the day he would flinch every time his phone rang, knowing a new deluge was about to begin. When he got home she would allow him some respite over dinner, and if he was lucky a game on the TV. As he sat and let the hard day fall away, Monica would slip off to her study nook beside the kitchen. This made him curious as she was doing it more and more. Jeremy would get up to go to the fridge and there she'd be, face blue as she peered into the glare of her computer monitor. Of course, Grady would be lying on the floor nearby. It looked like some sort of modern-day Norman Rockwell painting, only it didn't leave him feeling very sentimental.

He wanted badly to walk over and see exactly what it was she was reading, or searching for…he had a feeling she wasn't just surfing the net, or feeding an online shopping addiction. But he refused to exhibit any interest that might unleash a new wave of questions, so he'd inevitably make his way back to his chair, throw his feet up on the coffee table and grab the remote to do some surfing himself. The channels seemed to roll by one after another, and he was unable to concentrate as curiosity gnawed at the back of his mind.

Jeremy was becoming paranoid, and he didn't like it. Unfortunately though, he had good reason.

As the days went by Monica would lie down at night, thinking that her project hadn't pulled her and Jeremy closer, but was instead driving a wedge between them. The more she asked, the more he retreated. She decided to cut back on the pressure. The bedroom, bathroom and shower were off-limits.

After two weeks of slowly eroding their marriage, Monica learned the best way to get the information she needed was to find out from Shelly what Pepe was saying about the murders. It was no small irony that Shelly had little interest in police work, but had married a man who talked about it constantly. Pepe had likely guessed at the reason for Shelly's sudden, inexplicable interest, but Monica got the feeling he approved of her involvement. A qualified lawyer and hard worker, he'd be able to see the value in her help, even if her own husband couldn't.

Pepe realized that if Monica were going to help them with this case, she would need key information regarding the three murders, not just the snippets she gleaned from nights on the phone with Shelly. This meant crime scene photos, videos, transcripts, witness statements, and endless folders of paperwork, including the coroner's and autopsy reports.

Finally, Pepe cornered his partner and came straight out with it. "Are you going to give it to her, Jay?"

"When I get time, Pepe, when I get time," he said, jaw hardening. After a moment he added, "Hell, we got a serial killer to catch here. You and me are real detectives…this isn't some sort of family picnic!"

Pepe knew to back off, even if he felt they needed all the help they could get. Word was that Dorsey was going to go public with more information, and Pepe and Jeremy dreaded the press and public conjecture that would result, and likely bog down the investigation. The more knowledge the public had, the more whackos they'd have to deal with, making all kinds of claims. It made it that much harder for the detectives to differentiate between regular whack-jobs and the real one going around strangling people.

Once those kinds of leads started coming through Monica's assistance would be even more invaluable, but Pepe knew he had to tread lightly.

"Let me give a little info to Monica, just to keep her off your back." He raised his hands, as if to show he came into the conversation unarmed. "What can it hurt? She gets to be happy, you get all her lovin', and I don't have to listen to your bitching."

Jeremy's blue eyes hardened, as if an internal argument was raging inside that Pepe could only sense, rather than understand.

"No," he said finally. "She's my wife Pepe, and I'll tell her what I want to, when I want to, OK?"

Pepe had to work hard to keep his smile in place. "Sure bro, of course."

# CHAPTER TWENTY-NINE

For all her newfound distractions, Monica's garden seemed to benefit from her lack of attention, exploding with blooms and growth. She noticed this first in her white plumeria, king mantle, pink dragon wind begonia and her favorite of all, the blue-eyed grass. Even the bees seemed to buzz louder, and brighter. Everything was thriving, herself included.

If only she could say the same about her husband.

Increasingly he came home so late, his dinner was left in the oven for him to eat in front of the television alone. They no longer joked about his escapades at work, or moments throughout his day, as if he was afraid of introducing any subject related to his investigation. When he was at home, he sometimes made phone calls he didn't want Monica to hear, closing the bedroom door when she passed to use the bathroom. And when she tried to talk to him about the drug lords he'd shot, he grew angry, shutting down the conversation before it could begin.

She wanted to believe that his strange behavior had started when she approached him about wanting to get a job of some sort. Knowing the cause of his behavior would make it easier for her to devise a solution, some way to make him feel better again. Perhaps her job request had only made a bad situation worse...his detachment had begun after the shootings, after all.

When the four of them had met up that night, Jeremy had sat with his arm on the back of Monica's chair, resting his hand on her neck as they listened to Pepe recount the day's events with characteristic showmanship. His celebratory mood was understandable, as only a slight twist of fate could have resulted in a much darker outcome.

But for all the light hearted conversation, Jeremy sat tight lipped and frowning, his hand continuing its slow stroke at the nape of her neck. Monica grew melancholy at the thought of what dark matter must have been simmering inside him, or worse, the apparent lack of any emotion at all. Was that the man she'd married, someone incapable of feeling? And if so, could she blame him, dealing with what he did?

She started going down a list in her mind as she filled the pot up with her Columbian coffee and water from the Culligan jug that was delivered every Tuesday. She poured the water in the coffee maker, placed the carafe in the appropriate place, flipped the switch on, and automatically reached for something to read. On the top of the pile was a colorful coupon book, and she found herself leafing through the different offers, without registering a single one.

*He shows no anger, disappointment, or fear. In fact, the only time he exhibits real emotion is when he's with me, and frustrated by something I've done.*

They'd had a whirlwind romance, and she'd really gotten to know him over what was in hindsight, a short engagement period. *Know him.* The words hit her like a dropped clay flowerpot, full of dirt. She thought about their early days again, and wondered if she'd really ever gotten to know him. They had only dated for three months, and she'd been so taken by him that she didn't really think about the possibility of loving him, she simply did. And he loved her too, she knew that. But the advantage he had was that he knew whom he loved. She'd shared all her fears, frustrations and weaknesses, her deepest secrets. All the things he didn't seem to feel he could trust her with.

She pushed the coupon book to one side as the coffee finished brewing. Soon Jeremy would be up and out of bed, and she wanted to have his breakfast ready so she could focus her full attention on him when he woke. For all the tension that existed between them, Monica was determined to maintain the small, important things. A smile over a shared cup of coffee, the requisite kiss before he headed out to work. First and foremost, she was his wife and friend, even if he couldn't see her as a partner.

Then the sound of the garage door opening sent a roll of tension down her spine. She put down the coffee cup and treaded lightly over to the edge of the kitchen, calling out towards the bedroom. "Jeremy? Someone's opened the garage door."

Monica knew Jeremy was only a few feet away, and that the door at the end of the corridor was locked and bolted. Still, strange sounds continued to come from behind the back door and she felt herself grow more frightened.

She called out toward the bedroom for Jeremy once again, Grady sitting on his haunches with head cocked, watching her in confusion. Some guard dog. Just as she was about to walk into the bedroom and rouse her husband, she heard the metallic sound of cogs and chain links rotating, signifying the garage door was now being closed. Monica raced to the kitchen window to see if she could see anything outside.

"Jeremy!" she yelled.

Monica needed him and he was ignoring her. Someone could be breaking into the house and Jeremy was deciding that now was the time to make a point? Monica's hands trembled as she pulled open the door to their bottom oven. Attached to the top was a snub-nosed .38 caliber Smith and Wesson. Jeremy had disconnected the wiring in the back of the unit so it could not be mistakenly turned on, heating the loaded pistol.

On the one hand she knew she was being ridiculous, that there was every chance it was only Pepe, or some neighbor dropping by to return the lawn mower. On the other hand, cops tended to accumulate enemies, and so most friends knew that entering an officer's house without knocking would likely result in staring down the barrel of a gun, as Monica intended to illustrate.

The garage door had reached its final destination and shut completely. She peered out the window holding the .38 away from her right hip, with her finger extended on the outside of the trigger ring. Unfortunately the window was angled in such a way that she couldn't see past the box hedge separating the garden from the driveway.

Turning back, Monica noticed that Grady was intent on watching her and not the kitchen door. Usually strange noises made him alert, and it seemed both her men were letting her down today. With the gun gripped firmly in one hand Monica began to walk to the bedroom to force Jeremy to do something. The back door loomed at her like a jack-in-a-box about to spring open, and it was then she noticed something she missed before. The dead bolt was unlocked.

Someone must have entered through the front of the house while she was out jogging; that door could only be unlocked from inside. The fear curled inside her until it hardened into something wilder, a temporary insanity that made her heart beat against her ribs.

Oh God, what if Jeremy hadn't answered her call because someone had hurt him while she was out?

She curled her finger around the trigger, so scared she was almost afraid to breathe. The gun was out in front of her body, but she didn't know where to point it. She willed herself to take a deep breath and regain control of her thoughts. *Slow down, slow down.*

She looked back at Grady. *Why aren't you barking!* Instead he was completely relaxed, and almost looked as if he had a smile on his face.

Still clutching the gun, Monica whispered, "Are you laughing at me, Grady?"

The two brown eyes looked back up at hers, and with the flooding realization of a light bulb flickering on in a darkened room, she started to put two and two together.

The fear may have now turned to conviction, but the adrenalin still raced in her system as she sat the gun down on the kitchen island and walked briskly to the garage door. Monica gripped the handle and yanked it open, standing in the doorway with her hands on her hips and feet slightly spread, with all the bravado of Wonder Woman. Inside, she was anything but.

Jeremy's car was gone, his breakfast untouched and her cheek left unkissed for the first time in five years. Stupidly, she'd thought it more likely the house were under attack, than the possibility her husband might leave for work without saying goodbye. And while she'd been out of her mind with worry for his safety, he'd simply left for the day, with no thought of her at all.

Jeremy was gone.

# CHAPTER THIRTY

Detective Pepe Torentez sat behind a metal desk facing the only window in his office. It didn't offer a view of swaying palms, or sidewalk busy with people showcasing the latest in Miami fashion. Instead, his eyes were assaulted by cheap, wrinkled sport coats, white and blue button-downs, and to top it off...polyester neckties hanging loose at the front of each collar.

Whoever designed the corner office to overlook the detective quarters, with the back wall forever closed to a smorgasbord of sunshine and tanned bodies, sure had one sick sense of humor. The large square of glass was at least equipped with a venetian blind for privacy's sake, but after fifteen years of suffering the frustrations of three police chiefs, it hung off its frame looking as battered as Pepe felt.

A man of routine, Pepe would shut his office door with just enough force to let everyone outside know that he was in no mood to be bothered. This gesture was quickly followed by a tight yank of the blind, and the satisfying rattle of the metal strips unfurling all the way to the filing cabinets beneath. It took lots of practice to get it just right, and Pepe'd had lots of practice.

On this morning however his routine had been interrupted, as nine detectives awaited him in the meeting room. Problem was, there should have been ten.

He walked into the room and closed the door behind him with his signature slam. Turning, Pepe went to grab a doughnut from the plates in the middle and was met instead with...a banana.

"What the hell?"

One of the young pups at the front looked up at him nervously.

95

"Er, this is healthier, Chief." Then, clearly put off by the steam exiting Pepe's ears, "You know, to help us catch babes, as well as criminals?"

"I'm married," Pepe said, glancing at the small paunch that had appeared soon after his 31st birthday. "I reserve the right to get fat, OK?"

The collective snorts of laughter were silenced by his glare, and Pepe moved on to the business of the day: new leads relating to the serial killings. As they went around the table covering the various witnesses and family members who'd been interviewed, Pepe couldn't help but grind his teeth and wonder where his partner had disappeared to. Worse, it was clear to him that everyone in the department had taken note of his increasing absences as well. It was common knowledge that Jeremy was Pepe's best friend as well as partner, and it was safe to assume that many of the faces before him were thinking that Harlan was enjoying special treatment.

Pepe was not only the commander of their department, but Detective Harlan as well. It put Pepe in a position he didn't like at all. How could he expect any of these men to respect him if he couldn't get his own partner to show up for a debrief?

Presentation concluded, Pepe grabbed the folder in front of him and turned to leave, pausing to address the men.

"Good debrief. Rameros you'll send the notes to Monica Harlan?" The young officer nodded. "And I am sure Mr. Harlan will have a lot to offer when he does decide to join us, since he's working so *hard* and such *long* hours."

This was met with some laughs, but the men seemed to be watching him intently, as if he had a smear of ketchup on his cheek. "This is a sombrero full of shit," he grumbled, slamming the door once more behind him.

As Pepe walked towards his office he could hear them filing out of the meeting room, but at the back of his mind, something seemed off. They were moving too quickly. He wondered if his coat or pants were torn, or if there was a sign on his back or something. If Jeremy had been around, Pepe would have assumed he was the butt of some practical joke, having fallen victim to them so many times before. But his partner was yet to make an appearance.

Pepe's anger seemed to intensify along with the whispers, and the soles of his shoes slapped across the linoleum as he retreated to the safety of his office. He could think of nothing else but being pissed at Jeremy, and whatever his moronic men were worked up about. They probably expected him to jump on the phone and have a domestic with Jeremy, while they sat outside the glass box with bowls of popcorn. Well, he wouldn't give them the satisfaction.

Entering his office with the folder pinned beneath his arm, one hand grabbed the doorknob, while the other reached for the string hanging off the venetians, ready to execute his well practiced door-blind maneuver.

But instead of gripping string, he felt nothing.

His arm stretched… searching for the cord, the movement increasingly frantic, while the detectives watched on and burst into laughter.

When Pepe looked up, it finally sunk in. At the top of the blinds was a frayed string…it had been cut. And he knew exactly who had cut it.

He turned looking out the window feeling like he was on TV, the guys continuing to yuck it up. Some were high-fiving, others had their wallets and money clips out, paying off bets. From the collective celebrations, he gathered the blind had been severed for close to three days, with only three detectives guessing he'd make it to the end of the week.

But this was not the day to mess with Pepe Torentez. This was simply not the day.

He looked up at the window blind, locked permanently in place, and reached up. With a violent tug he ripped the entire shade down, the brackets popping right out of the plaster. As the blinds tumbled to the ground the officers were silenced by the crash of metal and plastic.

Gathering the mess up in his arms, Pepe pulled the door to his office open, letting it hit the wall so hard it bounced back enough to close again. He kicked it with all his might back to the wall, and once again it came flying back at Pepe fast enough to knock him over. But this was not met with laughter, only a sense of collective shock. Finally, the rebounding door slammed behind him and he managed to shuffle out.

He had everyone's attention now.

With the shades rattling and twisting, he carried them over and slammed them on top of Jeremy's desk, dumping them over his papers, phone, computer and lamp.

As Pepe walked back to his office he could hear the blinds dragging the contents of the desk onto the floor in a never-ending waterfall of clutter. As he reached his office door he opened it and screamed, *"Maldita sea!"* Even those who didn't speak Spanish could guess this wasn't an endearment.

His hand automatically reached for the blind string just as before…and the central office erupted into laughter once more.

Pepe would kill Jeremy, if he ever showed up.

# CHAPTER THIRTY-ONE

*Ding.*

The chime came from the nook in the corner of Monica's kitchen, which contained a small desk built into the wall, with two cabinet doors above and a single drawer beneath the writing area. Below the cabinet doors hung a single row of mail slots, a place to store bills, cards, letters, receipts, recipes and things of that nature.

She liked the little cubbyhole and the way it made her feel. Monica was not a fan of big spaces, having spent her entire childhood—at least the parts she remembered—in a huge bedroom with Gloria's awful makeup dresser. She tried to forget about those days, but now and again her mind would draw her back, and some of the memories were happy ones.

By the age of eleven or twelve, she'd had Alton wrapped around her little finger. She could look at him with her big brown eyes and pout her lip, and he would do anything to comfort her. Having said that, he never once tried to buy her love or affection with presents, only the true gold of his heart, and time.

But, as soon as she felt any sort of empathy for him, it was quickly vaporized by his marital choice. Love him as she did, Monica simply couldn't bring herself to respect a man who'd married a woman like Gloria. She might go as far as forgiving him for the mistake, but to *stay* married to her was irreconcilable.

Monica rarely got time alone with Alton. Gloria made sure no woman, not even their adopted daughter, got too close. But there was one day Monica remembered well, when she almost persuaded Alton to tell her who her real parents were.

Alton was in the house alone. Well, save for the maids, chef, and of course Monica's 'personal assistant'. But to anyone in that house, 'alone' really meant that the dragon had left her cave to go harass the villagers.

Monica made her way down the stairs and turned toward the big library looking for Alton. He was usually in this room smoking his pipe. She had developed a genuine fondness for the smell of Alton's tobacco smoke, almost as much as Alton had a fondness for smoking it.

Monica stood at the entrance to his magnificent study, watching her stepfather puff away. The smoke gently floated across the room, seeming to brush up the chandelier and then vanish into the ceiling. Alton would smile out of the corner of his mouth, still gripping the pipe with his teeth.

"Monica, my dear, come in."

Monica smiled as she stepped from the marble floor onto the Oriental rug. She was barefoot, but only because she knew Gloria wasn't home.

She didn't speak as she slid into one of the four leather chairs facing the unlit fireplace. Monica loved the feel of the leather and always sat in the same seat; the first on the left. She, unlike Gloria, never desired being the center of attention, though from the day she had arrived in that house she had somehow managed to be.

"Monica, do you know why I smoke this pipe?"

She peered up at him. "Because it tastes good?"

Alton laughed and walked over to the chair next to hers. He sat down, took the pipe out of his mouth and looked it over, as if seeing it for the first time.

"Not at all," he said. "I smoke this damn thing…" He caught his words and cleared his throat. "I smoke this, *thing*…" he repeated, "because Gloria hates it." A huge grin spread across his face as Monica giggled. As soon as she felt it escape her lips, she placed her hand over her mouth, embarrassed, but was quickly relieved when Alton burst out with an even greater laugh. Monica removed her hand, and the two of them giggled away, as if someone had released the pressure valve on an air tank.

They'd made so much noise that the maids came in to see what the matter was. When Monica told them about what had occurred her own giggles grew so contagious that soon the entire room full of adults was lost to a bout of hysterics.

To Monica, it was the single greatest day of her childhood.

After the staff had enjoyed their fill of amusement they trickled back to their duties. It was rare for anyone in that home to share such hilarity, and all of them felt somewhat privileged, even if the realization was tinged with sadness.

Still laughing a bit, and looking around to make sure they were once more alone, Monica said, "I hate the pipe too Alton, but I always come down here when you light it because I know it means Gloria's gone out."

She felt so good saying that, as if finally admitting it aloud removed a huge weight from her small chest. The admission still made her nervous, but because of what Alton had said, she knew she'd been given permission to speak her mind. It felt wonderful, like she had a teammate.

They continued to chat until Alton's smile had shrunk back to the usual frown, as if a thousand conflicting thoughts were racing around his mind. Monica realized that, caught in this moment of intimate distraction, now might be her best chance at getting the answer to a question that had plagued her ever since she was old enough to look in the mirror, and register the tan color of her skin.

Tentatively, Monica asked Alton if he might tell her who her really mommy and daddy were.

Alton's eyes cleared instantly, and he looked at her with an intensity she'd never seen before. Had she made a mistake in asking him?

"What did you just call me?"

"Call you?" she said, confused. "Nothing, Alton."

He scooted closer to the edge of his seat, and took her small hand in his own. "I thought I heard you call me, 'Daddy'."

Monica felt a flush cover her cheeks as she wondered what to say. Why would she call him 'Daddy', when he was only her carer? Gloria reminded her of the fact on an almost daily basis.

"I was only asking you who my mommy and daddy were, Alton."

101

He sat back in his chair, dropping her hand. To Monica, it almost seemed he was…disappointed, but to Monica this didn't make much sense. Still, she had questions that needed to be answered.

"Do you know, Alton? Do you know who they are?"

Alton fumbled with his pipe, thinking. After an almost unbearable silence, he gave a long, drawn out sigh, and began to speak. Monica's heart hammered in her chest.

"Gloria and I used to go on holidays to a place call—"

"*Monica!*"

Gloria stood, fuming in the doorway. "Where are your shoes?"

Walking over, she scowled at the small feet, propped up against the leather. "Get up to your room this instant, and put them on."

Monica looked at Alton, and Alton looked away.

"We don't want Beverly *Hillbillies* running around our home. Do we?"

Monica cast a final look at her protector, and pulled a piece of gum from her pocket, taking out her frustration with the frantic working of her jaw.

"Now, young lady!"

She stood up, brushing past the dragon.

"And spit out that gum. Nice girls do not chew like that!"

*Pop! Pop-pop!*

Monica made sure Gloria could hear her bubbles echoing through the foyer, and fifteen years later she found herself standing in the kitchen, still chewing away.

*Ding!*

There it was again.

She had forgotten about the noise and made her way over to her laptop, waiting patiently in the nook.

# CHAPTER THIRTY-TWO

Monica eased herself in to the computer chair and placed her cup of green tea on the backside of an envelope, as Grady relocated himself from kitchen stool to the space in front of her feet. He was far too small to fit under the desk, but apparently he'd never realized he was no longer a puppy.

Monica felt a small thrill as the screensaver cleared to reveal an instant message from *Pepepossum*. This usually meant fresh details from the investigation.

*Pepepossum: Can't find your husband, and after this morning's fun I'm ready to arrest him myself. What are you guys doing? Knock it off, finish up...Tell him to get his ass in here right now, would ya?*

*Gradysmom: Morning Pepe. Jeremy left a while ago. I think we're fighting...*

*Pepepossum: You think you are?*

*Gradysmom: Yeah, he left this morning without saying bye, or touching his breakfast. I think the case might be starting to get to him.*

Monica could almost feel Pepe through the screen, reading her words and worrying about his partner. Eventually, he replied.

*Pepepossum: The job gets to everyone at some point. Don't worry. Are you ready for some more leads?*

Monica smiled and answered in the affirmative. For the past week she had met Pepe online at least once a day, and sometimes more. Jeremy had not held up his end of the deal, and so she felt no disloyalty in turning to his partner for help instead. Pepe had been reluctant at first, eventually giving in after a few harsh words from Shelly. Life around the Torentez house had not been pleasant of late, which wasn't helping their attempts at bringing a new little Torentez into the world.

*Pepepossum: You have everything so far on the first two vics. Here is what I have on the third. Ready?*

*Gradysmom: Yep.*

*Pepepossum: Debra Wright. This is the first victim who lived outside of Dade County, but she was found in Coral Gables, outside the Lowe Art Museum.*

*Gradysmom: Age? Height? Weight? What was she dressed like?*

*Pepepossum: Similar to the other women. Age 29. 5'6, 133 lbs. I'll send you images of the clothing.*

*Gradysmom: Strangulation? No defensive wounds again?*

*Pepepossum: Exactly the same. All but the age, and this girl was maybe a bit fitter than the others.*

*Gradysmom: She didn't fight back?*

*Pepepossum: Doesn't look like it. She was wearing crocs, the back straps were over the top of each shoe. No way they would stay on during a struggle.*

*Gradysmom: Security cameras outside the museum?*

*Pepepossum: Yes, and just like the others, not a single one with an angle on where the body was found.*

Monica paused as the facts settled in, and a moment later a file appeared in her email.

She scrunched up into a ball in her chair, her knees to her chest and notebook on top of her knees. She had a book for each victim, and would write, lean over, and reach around her knees as she continued to type, messaging her thanks to Pepe as he signed off.

Monica wrote frantically, her mind racing back to the details of the first two victims. The report Pepe had sent didn't reveal much in addition to what he's said in his messages, except for the fact that the murder weapon was about one inch thick and made of nylon. As soon as she had written this down, she grabbed the other two notebooks and compared them against one another.

A final message popped onto the screen.

*Pepepossum: You should also know this victim was not married and she worked at a cosmetic counter for Este Lauder. She had no roommates.*

Monica reached around her knees and answered.

*Gradysmom: Have you been to her place? House or apt.?*
*Pepepossum: Jeremy and I were going to get over there yesterday but never did…Will most likely go today.*
*Gradysmom: Can I go!!!*
*Pepepossum: I don't see why not, if your boy don't care, I don't care. But don't touch anything.*
*Gradysmom: Pepe you punk! You know I know the drill…LAWYER over here, hello?*
*Pepepossum: I know, I know...*
*Gradysmom: What time?*
*Pepepossum: I'll have Jay-man call you, assuming he shows up. Around 3?*

Monica was nervous. She was thinking that the less Jeremy was involved in this decision, the better her chances were on going.

*Gradysmom: How about I show up around 2 and if we go, we go??*
*Pepepossum: Cool chica…cya*

And with that, Monica was left to spend the morning picturing Jeremy's face as she waltzed into the precinct. This was going to be fun.

# CHAPTER THIRTY-THREE

Monica caught herself calling the woman by her given name, but she knew better than that. She'd been taught to call them "victims" or "vics", as this was supposed to keep things from getting too personal. She tried to say it over again in her head, but the name 'Debra Wright' kept dominating her thoughts, so she gave up.

She had the same problem with the first three names.

Vic #1, Hanna Gallaway, found at Kirk Munroe Park.

Monica had written on the outside of the green notebook, *Victim One*, but even as she opened the spiral notebook her mind whispered, *Hanna*. She stared at the pages with her notes written in pencil, and surrounded by small sketches of all sorts of things. The style of a shoe, or piece of jewelry. There was nothing gruesome or gory about these murders, aside from the horror of death itself. Monica had seen plenty of gore from her past experiences in law school and while completing her internship for the district attorney of Miami Dade County. And yet her own drawings disturbed her more than those photos had. It was all becoming strangely personal.

Monica now had four notebooks, one for each victim, plus an additional black one where she'd laid out a comparison chart for the three, trying to find similarities and differences between the murders.

Hanna, or *the vic*, had been killed between the hours of 7:00P.M. and 8:30P.M. on a Sunday, the date being September seventh. She laid the green notebook down and fished for the red one, which bore "Victim Two" on the cover, but again whispered the name *Daleena Mendez*.

106

On the notebook paper Monica had drawn a picture of a young woman sipping coffee while seated near the street, on a patio at a coffee shop. A waiter stood nearby, and a dog like Grady was at her feet.

She ran her thumb over Daleena's face for a moment and then traced up the page to rest on the highlighted reference, TOD. It read 8:15–9:00P.M. She closed the red notebook and opened the blue, grabbing the black Sharpie next to her computer and writing "Debra Wright" across the front. Just as she had finished the last letter she realized what she'd done.

She hurried her mind along, adding "Victim Three" in smaller letters below, and began to switch back and forth between the notebooks. It appeared all the murders had taken place on Sunday evenings, and maybe more importantly, that all had occurred on the first Sunday of each month, beginning from October. She tried to make a connection in her mind as to the significance, and wondered if it might be related to the Church in some way, or a specific kind of work schedule.

Next, she made a note of each of the locations where the bodies had been found. Hanna Gallaway, the first victim, found at Kirk Munroe Park on Florida Avenue.

Daleena Mendez, victim two, found at Rockway Pool and Park on SW Twenty-seventh Drive between SW Ninety-fifth Avenue and SW Twenty-seventh Street.

Debra Wright, victim three, found near the Lowe Art Museum five miles directly south of Miami.

Monica made a note that all were dressed casually, which busted her Church theory apart. She knew this meant something important, but had no clue what that might be. She had asked Pepe if any of the victims had been jogging; what type of shoes they'd been wearing and if there'd been traces of excessive sweating before death. The answer had been no.

So, why were all these girls in parks and open spaces, if they weren't there to exercise? This brought her to what she thought to be the most curious of circumstances surrounding the murders. The victim's cars had all been found nearby, but none of the bodies had car keys on them, and so far, none of the keys had been located. Their purses and IDs were also missing. One could only assume the killer took all of these, and cleaned each car out, leaving only the license plate and VIN's to trace identities. *Had the murderer locked the vehicles?* Monica jotted this down as a question for Pepe, and scanned the others she had written, with each carefully numbered. There was a total of one hundred and twelve queries. She noticed some she had written down twice, and others were not questions so much as possible scenarios.

Monica harbored great doubts about her ability to help at all with the investigation, faced with so many questions and yet to discover a single answer. Knowing where to start was one of the greatest challenges, and Monica felt a weight settle on her shoulders. It was heavy, too heavy it seemed, and cloaked in helplessness.

What could she really do?

She put her pencil down for the moment and popped a gum bubble, then reached for the Sharpie again. With deliberate, almost frustrated strokes, she crossed out the text on the covers of the green and red notebooks, and replaced them with names instead. Now the three covers sat next to one another on the table.

Hanna Gallaway

Daleena Mendeza

Debra Wright

She rested her chin on her hand, the lamp from her desk bathing the lower half of her face in light. When Monica dropped the sharpie and drifted back to her pencil, her hand continued on to a blank sheet of paper as if of its own desire. Eyes glazed she worked in a trance, and was almost surprised to find the sketch materialize into a man sitting on a bench…a park bench. She brought more detail to the face, the hair, nose and eyes, and a final, small cleft in the chin, only to stop suddenly; her pencil grinding to a halt and the tip snapping off and bouncing across the page.

Monica knew that face anywhere.

# CHAPTER THIRTY-FOUR

Pepe had been waiting at the precinct for either Jeremy or Monica to show up, and while his partner had never managed to make an appearance, he had at least phoned Pepe to let him know he was with Al down at the medical examiner's office.

Pepe's first instinct was to tell Jeremy that Monica would be joining them at the third victim's apartment at Sea Ranch Lakes, but Jeremy never really gave him the chance.

"Hey man, I'm going to grab a quick workout after I leave Al here, and then I'll head over to Sea Ranch. See you there at three?"

"Sure bro, bu—"

Jeremy had already hung up. Pepe stared at the phone in his hand and wondered if he should call back, before deciding that Jeremy's abruptness had actually made life easier for him. If he just showed up with Monica in the car, what could Jeremy say then? He tried his best to rehearse the conversation, only to shrug and accept that when the shit hit the fan, he'd have to duck and cover.

Monica showed up at the precinct early. Things always went quiet when she appeared, gliding between the desks in tight jeans and a T-shirt that, no matter the size, fit snugly across certain parts of her figure.

Playfully, Pepe held out his arms and said, "Mamita!"

Monica smiled. With her sunglasses raised over her forehead, she embraced Pepe in a brotherly hug and replied, *"Caramba, de perlas!"*; an affectionate expression of "Wow, just what someone needs!"

The young woman did an admirable job of ignoring the many sets of eyes that were fixated upon her as they walked towards the doors.

"Are you sure you're up for this?"

"Yes."

She looked around the space, as if searching for someone.

"He's down at the M.E.'s office, said he was going for a workout before meeting us at the vic's."

Monica's shoulders slumped, but she nodded at Pepe, as if almost relieved.

Turning left off North Ocean Drive, Monica could see Jeremy's car parked outside the house. "Jeremy must be inside," she said to Pepe.

She was not taking in any details concerning the victim's residence, as she knew she should have been; her thoughts instead diverted to the impending confrontation with her husband.

Pepe shrugged. "He will be outside somewhere, if I know him. Jeremy is always looking beyond the tape."

They parked the car and got out, walking toward the front of the house and passing through a pair of tall hibiscus shrubs that framed the entry gate. Suddenly a voice came from right behind Monica's ear, close enough so she could feel the breath. She jumped away, even as she recognized it almost immediately.

"Jeremy Harlan, you scared me to death!"

Jeremy stood over her, calm and still as a pillar of stone. "Scared of your own husband?" he asked sarcastically. "Nancy Drew-riguez…you're meant to be a better detective than that."

The words were harsh, but Monica knew they were only masking his surprise, and probable hurt, at her unexpected appearance.

Jeremy swung his expressionless face around and managed a slight grin for Pepe.

"You didn't tell me we had a new partner today."

"*A mi modo de ver amigo,*" Pepe started, continuing in English, "I tried to tell you earlier before, but you hung up." Hands in open in supplication, he finished with, "*No armar una bronca!*"

Jeremy looked back at Monica and sighed. "Damn, I can tell you guys have been hanging out together. Mowgli, what in the hell did Pep just say?"

Monica instantly felt a bit more at ease. Early into their marriage Jeremy had given her that nickname, saying she looked like the small, brown character from *"The Jungle Book"*. They both knew she loved it.

Smiling, she answered "He said he was sorry, and that I made him bring me."

This was a total lie, Pepe telling Jeremy that he needed a little perspective, and that he didn't want a fight. Monica knew well that Jeremy was familiar with the actual words for "I'm sorry," having used them many times at the start of their relationship, usually after rolling through the door at the end of a long night with Pepe and the boys.

Jeremy narrowed his eyes and Pepe changed the subject. "Have you been inside?"

"No, the entrance is over there, on the west side."

With that, he turned and walked around the side of the house where the driveway was located. There was a wrought iron set of stairs that led to an apartment above the garage. "Nothing at all out here," commented Jeremy. "I mean nothing."

Pepe took the lead, seemingly anxious to get to the staircase. Monica stayed safely behind them, listening and watching. As was often the case she found herself paying more attention to Jeremy than her surroundings, and tried to slow down and study things. But Monica had never worked a crime scene, or visited a victim's house. She had no idea what to look for, or not look for, so she decided she'd try to make the most of her natural intuition, and pretend to embody Debra by walking in her shoes, feeling what she might have felt that day. Standing at the door, it suddenly seemed ridiculous, even though it had sounded good in her mind on the drive over.

Again her focus shifted to Jeremy. He seemed so strange to lately, or was it only that she was the one changing? Did she also seem strange to him? Monica tried to convince herself the latter was the greater possibility, but the anxiety remained.

# CHAPTER THIRTY-FIVE

Pepe removed a pocket knife from his pants pocket and cut through the police sticker stuck to the doorjamb. Folding the blade closed and popping it back into his front pocket, he slipped the key inside the door and with a quick turn, opened it. Pepe walked in first, followed by Monica. Jeremy remained on the staircase landing surveying the yard around the home.

"Take your time Monica, take it all in, and tell us if you find anything worth noting."

Monica was barely moving at all, more swaying from side to side in the tiny living area. It felt strange, as if she was robbing a grave or violating someone's secret place. The life of Debra Wright surrounded her.

She leaned over a small side table to study a series of photos displayed in all sorts of colorful frames.

"It's okay to pick the photos up and look at them," said Pepe. "Just don't touch anything unusual that could become evidence."

Monica took a photo in her hand and raised it closer to her face. "It just seems so strange to see all of this and know this person is gone."

The photo was of Debra and what looked to be a close friend, the two young women reclining at the beach. It struck Monica that life was only a sequence of moments, and that photos served to freeze them. But once they were gone, they were gone. This particular one touched something inside her bone deep, and her fingers trembled as she stared at the two girls soaking up life on what looked like a very hot day, both wearing big smiles and sunglasses.

Debra Wright was the victim in this crime, but it could have been any one of her friends, heaven forbid Shelly or even herself. This gave her an eerie feeling, one that she hoped was not a premonition of any kind.

She placed the photo back and continued to look around, vaguely aware of Pepe and Jeremy talking on the landing.

"I looked in the fridge, the bathroom and the medicine cabinet," said Pepe. "I can't find anything that might link this one with the others."

"I've been trying to tell you, Pepe," responded her husband, "there ain't nothing at any of these girls' homes that offers a link. It's going to be someone they work with, someone who knows them, from a gym or a coffee shop. Hell, maybe we just got ourselves a guy who picks them up in a bar?"

"Picks 'em up in a bar? How do you convince some girl in a bar to drive her own car to a public park or museum that early in the evening? All the vics were killed before ten or eleven o'clock." Pepe's voice seemed frustrated. "Al said no alcohol, so that says to me, no bar."

"Well, we ain't getting nothin' done here."

Monica could hear the solid thump of Jeremy's boots down the steps.

"Where you going, *vato*?" called Pepe.

The rhythmic thumping continued, then faded off.

"*Hey!* Where you going?"

"Home to my wife, Pepe!" he shouted, adding a moment later, "oh that's right, she's a cop now!"

Monica heard a car door slam, and sensed Pepe walking back inside.

"Are you all right?" he asked.

"Yes of course. He's just blowing off steam." A small simmer of frustration made her clench her hands. She could understand Jeremy's frustration with their relationship, but to storm off, as if the investigation itself was of no importance to him. He acted like he didn't even want to find the killer, making smart comments and disappearing every five minutes.

A cool, steely sense of resolution settled inside her. If Jeremy didn't want to investigate this case properly, she would.

"I need to see the other homes. Hanna Gallaway's and Daleena Mendez's." Then, with authority, "Tonight."

Pepe's eyebrows shot straight up. "*Tonight*, tonight?"

Monica smiled. "As Jeremy would say, 'sleep when you're dead', Pepe."

# CHAPTER THIRTY-SIX

Jeremy took his time driving back from Sea Ranch; there was no point battling the traffic back toward the Intracoastal Waterway down around Hallandale. This was home to Arlo's, and he couldn't get there fast enough. He needed a drink.

Cruising by the palm trees as he had a million times before, he thought back to the first time he'd laid eyes on Monica, at Pepe and Shelly's rehearsal dinner. He and Pepe had been working in uniform back then, and had showed up at the country club in their blues. Jeremy was not looking forward to the inevitable boring conversations, mulling over which fork was for the salad, and whether the big knife was for buttering his bread.

Back in his college football days, being named All-SEC for three straight years had made him the best man of choice for close to a dozen weddings. It was one of the reasons he'd moved as close to the 'real' south as he could.

Jeremy recalled hiding out in the church when the wedding director called out his name.

He was all too familiar with the routine; do whatever she says, no matter how stupid, cheesy, or girlie. This was Pepe's wedding, the closest thing he had to a brother. Of course, this wouldn't stop him from pulling at least a dozen practical jokes on the groom before the celebrations were through, but he could at least stand up and play his part when told to.

He'd heard his name called a second time and walked towards a lady with big hair and wire glasses perched on the tip of her nose. Cutting her eyes up at him, she made it clear she recognized trouble when she saw it coming, even if she did straighten her blouse and stand a little straighter.

"Jeremy?"

"Yes ma'am."

The words had a sort of melting effect, as he knew they would, and the woman smiled, lashes fluttering as she looked back down at the clipboard in her hands. She wasn't the only woman who'd been affected by his deep, warm voice. Like birds on a wire, the bridesmaids seated in the second pew turned as if on command, a young Monica Howard sitting in the centre.

Jeremy remembered the moment. He had never been very comfortable with his good looks, but he had learned to use them to advantage.

"Monica Howard?" The wedding director had found her voice once more. "Monica? Who's Monica?" She narrowed her eyes as a beautiful Latina lady exited the pew to join them.

"Monica, you will be escorted by this fine officer." The words were professional, if a little choked.

"Howdy, ya'll don't mind me standing here do ya?"

Jeremy cocked a brow, ready to tell her to take her fake Southern accent and stick it where the sun might never find it, but paused. The two brown eyes looking up at his were liquid warmth, and his smart ass reply died on his lips.

Lost in the depths of his memory, Jeremy almost failed to miss the two red brake lights that suddenly appeared in front of him. He smashed his foot on the brake just in time to miss the Z-4 waiting at the intersection. Taking a deep breath, he pried his fingers from the steering wheel.

The truth was, Jeremy hadn't been worthy of such a perfect woman that day, and nothing much had changed in the five years since. He'd just had a fool's luck being in the right place at the right time, with a girl too sweetly naïve to know better.

The traffic was moving along at a quicker pace than before, and Jeremy's mind picked up speed as well. He couldn't help but feel a bit guilty about the way he'd left her in the morning, and then again just forty-five minutes ago. When she looked up at him with those big brown eyes, her confusion tinged with sadness, it made him feel like he'd kicked a puppy.

Monica deserved better. She deserved someone as perfect as herself, and Jeremy knew more than anyone how imperfect he truly was.

The trouble was in that in the last few months he'd felt consumed by his past, and drawn into the very darkest parts of who he was. Half the time he was on auto pilot, his actions barely thought out, and dangerous enough to risk everything he'd built in his life, career, friendship with Pepe, and his marriage. God, if they knew the full truth, the darkness that ran through his very DNA, would they even be able to look at him again?

He felt a huge wave of remorse settle over his entire body and suddenly felt trapped.

He needed air.

The window slid down and hot air brushed across his face. Reaching over, he turned up the radio, loud. The song was *"Start Me Up"* by the Stones, and he found himself tapping his hands against the steering wheel and singing, *"Once you start me up I never stop, never stop, never, never, never stop."*

Hearing them, a new meaning dawned that left him feeling disgusted and terrified at the same time. He reached to roll the other window down and turned the radio up even more, desperately trying to drown out his thoughts. How he wished it were all a dream, after all, it seemed so surreal.

But it had to stop.

It had to stop before Monica got hurt. And now that she had involved herself, it was only a matter of time before she discovered everything.

# CHAPTER THIRTY-SEVEN

At 11:45P.M., Pepe lowered himself into the car, weary after viewing the last of the victim's houses. At the second house he'd watched Monica pause and look at something on the floor, her face illuminated with inspiration. Pepe had asked her what she'd discovered, but she only waved her hand and said it was probably nothing. At the third house, she'd raced straight to the back porch, and smiled triumphantly. "What?" Pepe had said, but again she only shook her head.

Pepe started the engine. "Personally, I think you're just playing. Trying to act like you've found somethin' so you don't have to feel bad hauling my ass around town all night."

Monica folded her arms. "Maybe I just want to do a bit more research before I present my case, like any good lawyer."

He snorted. "Maybe you're gonna make up whatever suits you, like every lawyer." This brought about a quick tightening of her jaw.

"How long have you been a detective, Pepe?"

Pepe was used to hearing this question from his superiors, whenever he'd overlooked something obvious. His gut told him Monica might be onto something.

"What did I miss?" He said it as if he knew he was a dumb ass, encouraging her to go ahead and get her gloating over with.

"Well, Pepe, you are so busy at the moment, and I am sure you would have noticed this soon anyway. Or Jeremy, for that matter—"

"*Tener el alma en un hilo!*" he said. I'm on pins and needles!

Monica positioned herself so that she was facing him, her eyes bright and filled with excitement, and Pepe couldn't help but feel sad that Jerry was too damn stubborn to share in this moment.

When Monica finally revealed what she had found, he could only scratch his chin, in awe of her and kicking himself at the same time. It was as obvious as a dog with a bone.

# CHAPTER THIRTY-EIGHT

Faye had been selling real estate in Miami for over ten years, and was savvy when it came to giving out her e-mail address, or any personal details for that matter. She was constantly setting up appointments and meetings with strangers; it was part of her job. But she was well aware that there were some crazy people out there, and female realtors were prime targets for lonely men who might want to lure women into empty houses.

When she'd first started selling she'd had a partner, her husband Rolly. A man's presence had been a comfort when showing properties to a new client, and even when he couldn't make a viewing, he still looked vaguely threatening standing by her side on her business cards, and online. But Faye had been single and divorced for over five years, and these days she went it alone.

Fighting past her initial fears and reminding herself that she was a strong, empowered woman, Faye had developed a series of safety mechanisms. When speaking to a new client for the first time she got all the information she could, including telephone numbers for both home and work, testing them both to arrange and then confirm their meeting. She knew to do a reference check, even looking up tax records. And if she was at all concerned, she could ask her old college friend at the courthouse to do a background check. Faye would always meet the client out in a public place, if it was possible, and ask the client to ride with her to retain as much control as possible. She'd even pretend to be on the phone as she approached the waiting prospect, slipping her plans and the client's name into the end of her faux conversation to make it clear there were others who knew of her whereabouts.

Faye was so proud of her safety methods that she had actually started writing a book for realtors and women dating online, and was very excited about the project. She was successful in real estate and well known in the Miami area, attracted to the idea of becoming an expert, and helping other women out. Local women found themselves in strange times, independent and yet vulnerable, especially with a serial killer on the loose.

The realtor had no children, but if you asked Faye she would say she did, and pull out her iPhone to reveal a photo of a little white dog, with big black splotches on his forehead and left jaw.

"That's my boy, Jack. Isn't he precious?"

Faye had brought him home one month after her divorce was made final, and often wondered what she would have done without him in those early days. Heaven forbid he get hit by a car or ran away, there was no other dog-mom in the world more protective of her "baby" than Faye Bowman.

Ten days earlier Faye had flown to Houston, Texas, for a sales conference. Refusing to leave little Jack with any kennel she instead hired a pet sitter. Maria was wonderful with Jack, and Faye felt very good about him staying at home in his normal environment. Then, just as she'd been walking into the hotel foyer to register her attendance at the event and pick up her welcome bag, she'd seen Maria's name flash up on the screen and suffered a small jolt of apprehension. Ten minutes later she was standing on the street, suitcase in hand, and waving down a taxi to head back to the airport.

Apparently Maria had been walking Jack down the street when a bullmastiff had come up at them, almost out of nowhere.

"Why didn't you pick him up?" Faye had wailed.

"I wanted to, I did! But before I had a chance he'd slipped the collar."

This was Faye's fault. She hated him feeling constricted, so his collar was fixed loosely around his slender, brown neck. Usually that didn't matter as Jack behaved well on his leash, but when the mastiff brute had appeared, Jack had decided that being tied up was not going to aid his defense.

# The Lost Dog

According to Maria the small dog had risen up on his hind legs and bared his teeth as their attacker stood only a foot away, barking ferociously. Maria had looked around for an owner, a stick, anything, but had finally realized her only choice was to scoop the small dog up and probably lose an arm in the process. When she'd gone to do it, the mastiff had lunged and Jack had taken off through the shrubs, the big, black beast hot on his heels. A minute later she stood alone in the park, Jack's leash dangling from her fingers, the dog nowhere to be found.

When Faye arrived in Miami she drove around the neighborhood for hours, walking through the park and loudly shaking Jack's favorite box of doggie treats. That evening was spent making phone calls, putting up flyers and placing ads on a range of lost dog online forums and general community notice boards. The reward was substantial, enough for the local paper to agree to run a story, and she felt hopeful that—assuming Jack hadn't been mauled to death—someone would bring him home.

Just as she was about to finally collapse after twelve straight hours of tears, work, and then more tears, a notification grabbed her attention. With a small thrill of excitement she saw that it was from one of the lost dog sites, and the breath left her in a small, joyful gasp. The listing had only been live for two hours and already someone was trying to make contact. She clicked the message open, and clapped her hands in excitement.

# CHAPTER THIRTY-NINE

The working title for Faye's book was *"Stranger Survival Rules"*. Rule number ten was probably the most important of them all, and yet when the gentleman on the phone asked her to meet at a local park, she didn't even stop to think of the public café she usually assigned for such purposes. After all, he seemed well mannered enough and he was doing *her* a favor. He'd even made her laugh, telling her how he'd been driving through her neighborhood and noticed the small, scruffy dog wandering around without a collar. Then Jack's photo had appeared on elperroperdido.com.

Richard's deep, warm voice was pleasant, even charming, and Faye allowed herself to wonder what he might look like. After all, she was single and the man was obviously a dog lover, in fact, the way he talked about Jack Russells as a breed led her to think he might work in a pet related industry, or be a breeder. For a moment she was overcome with the image of herself sitting on a couch beside a tall, handsome man, a litter of brown and white puppies scrambling over their laps. She almost swooned.

"How about I meet you after work this evening? You must be missing Jack terribly…"

"Oh, just knowing he's safe is wonderful. I mean, if tonight is inconvenient at all—"

"It's fine," said Richard. "But as a cop, I'd encourage you to meet me in a public place. There are some strange people out there, and women need to be careful. Having said that, I wouldn't want you to turn up at *my* house wielding an axe, either!"

They both laughed.

"How about you meet me after I get off of my shift, say around 9:00P.M.?" Before she could agree, he'd already mapped out a plan. "I'll meet you at the Little River Park over off of NW Twenty-fourth Avenue. You can find it easily, and it's well lit."

All she had to do was go straight in and pull up to the outdoor basketball court. A pool would be on her right, and a pavilion directly in front where Richard would be waiting. Then he added that he played basketball in the police league, and Faye's image of puppies was dispersed by one of a slick, bare chest and broad brown hands, pumping a basketball up and down.

Swallowing her excitement, Faye wrote down everything he had said.

"What kind of car do you drive, so I know what to look for?"

"A white Mercedes."

"Great," he purred. "Make sure you bring Jack's leash, he's going to be really glad to see you."

As Faye turned her Mercedes into the entrance of the Little River Park, she couldn't believe she was about to be reunited with her baby. The listing had gone live and two hours later an alert had appeared. This had been followed by a phone call the next morning, and now—less than twenty-four hours later—the reunion she'd been waiting for so desperately. For the twentieth time that day she thanked God for modern technology, and the greatest blessing of all: the Internet.

Her eyes searched left and right looking for Jack, while her brain processed the directions Richard had passed on. Faye noticed the basketball courts on her left, but no one was playing on them, and the huge pool on her right seemed closed. Then her headlights lit up the large, white pavilion.

"This is it," she said aloud, heart beating.

For a brief moment, the words 'stranger' and 'survival' flashed across her mind, and she pictured herself on the cover of her book, arms crossed and face set in a stern expression. As she began to sense the multitude of rules she'd broken just by being there, she noticed the sedan parked behind the pavilion, and thought instead of what it would feel like to hold Jack in her hands once more, his round, smooth belly supported in her palm.

She got out of her car with his leash in hand.

The grass was quite tall and the blades tickled her ankles, cool and moist in the evening dew. Faye made a sharp turn around the northern corner of the pavilion and took about two steps more, her toes wet through the front of her open sandals. It was dark, and she couldn't see Jack or Richard anywhere, until she sensed someone behind her and heard the gentle rush of footsteps over soft vegetation. There was a prick at the back of her neck, like a mosquito bite, and she raised her hand to swipe at it, only to encounter another hand.

"Rich-"

As Faye turned her lips went numb, and a moment later her view of the park was obscured by the small forest of grass pressed against her lashes.

She could not speak, nor move her mouth, arms, or feet. But she could still see, and registered the bright green flash of Jack's leash as it slipped past her face. For a moment Faye wondered if she was having a stroke, then she noticed the shadow hovering around her, and remembered the women who'd been found, strangled. Her body was numb, but she could still feel the burn of suffocation, and hear the faint sound of music as she saw a much younger version of herself running across the grass. It was magnificent, reminding her of the opera her dad had taken her to as a child in New York.

And then, all was quiet.

He let her fall limp to the ground, tugged the leash from her throat and placed it inside his jacket. The keys to her Mercedes were in her pocket, and she carried no purse. They usually left their purses in the car, scared perhaps, of walking around with all that reward money in a strange place and meeting a strange person.

As he walked slowly back to her car the thrill of the past three minutes was so intoxicating that his motions had to be kept under tight control. *They all want a car like this.* Princesses, with their little dogs and castles in the sky.

He pushed the button on the key to unlock the car, but it was already open.

He figured it would be, reaching in with his latex gloves and removing her purse, as well as the directions lying on the seat. He wasn't sweating; he wasn't panicked at all. In fact, he was perfectly calm as he surveyed the inside of the car like a robot, taking in information and dismissing anything unnecessary, spitting it out of his mind as quickly as it was categorized.

He shut the car door and pressed the lock button before placing the keys inside the purse. Then he walked over to the only other car in the lot and got inside, firing the motor and driving past the Mercedes. His fingers tapped the steering wheel as he replayed those last minutes over and over again, fragments and details from the other women combining until they blended into a single, pulsing sensation of ecstatic power.

It felt like the electricity before the storm, the wonderful anticipation followed by the dark, heavy threat of nearby clouds, waiting to burst open and wreak their devastation. He loved every moment of it, the high and the risk, his own life and theirs as it ebbed away to nothing in his arms. He let himself feel genuine hate. He felt it deep within taking over and turning into a dark depression… He was not fulfilled. He was not satisfied.

He must do it again.

# CHAPTER FORTY

Monica couldn't wait to get home.

When Pepe pulled into the precinct parking lot she had her hand on the door latch before the car had even come to a stop. As the door slammed she heard something like "See y—", Pepe's words lost as her long legs raced to her red Mini Cooper. As Monica pulled up to their small beach house however, her enthusiasm waned. It was close to midnight and her intuition whispered that Jeremy would not be home.

She didn't let herself dwell on it; she figured he was over at Arlo's, probably drinking with the staff after closing. It wouldn't be the first time. Inside the garage, with Jeremy's car nowhere to be seen, she grabbed her Walgreens bag and purse, locked up and moved toward the kitchen door.

Thankfully the house was not the silent, lonely void she'd anticipated. Instead, a 105-pound welcoming committee awaited. Monica had never so glad to see Grady. He was wagging his tail as if fighting off an army behind him; the large, swinging club at his rear daring anyone to come too close. The only taker was the hallway hat stand, which came toppling towards Monica along with its collection of linen bags, caps and beach visors.

Once she had it upright once more and had deposited her own bags, she bent down to squeeze Grady's face, kiss his snout and massage his ears in a slow, rolling circle. The house was dark, and she realized with a pang how much she missed the dark blue jacket that usually hung beside her own, completing her hallway picture.

When the thrashing had slowed to a soft, contented thumping, she finally released Grady to go to the utility room in search of fresh water and a cup of biscuits. A moment later Grady's evening meal was in its place by drier, but his usual raging appetite was gone; the dog staring up at her with his eyebrows lifted. She had so much on her mind, she'd almost forgotten. "Oh, *lo siento*, baby."

She quickly exited the utility room with him right on her heels, and once the backdoor was open he'd launched himself out so quickly he almost sent her head over heels. She cast her eyes across the small garden, and the ocean beyond it, but instead of a sense of peace, the view left her feeling vaguely unsettled. She almost felt as if someone were watching her, and became instantly aware of the fact that while the beach was cloaked in the darkness of a new moon, she was standing in the bright light of her kitchen; an actor in the spotlight of a darkened stage. It made her feel vulnerable and exposed, and when Grady padded up to her and nudged his wet nose against her hand, she almost jumped out of her skin.

Chastising herself for being melodramatic, Monica slid the door shut and locked it behind her. In the nook beckoned her laptop, and while she knew she should go and get some rest she couldn't stop herself from moving the mouse and watching the desktop icons magically appear. She clicked on the icon titled, "*Asesino en Serie*". Serial Killer.

A new email blinked at the bottom of the screen and as she clicked open the message from Pepe she felt a cool wave of dread settle in her bones.

They had found another body.

It was late, so Pepe hadn't called, but in the hour since she'd left him in the precinct car park the call had come in, as well as a positive I.D.

Faye Bowman had been thirty-nine years old, five-three and around 120 pounds, a well regarded real-estate broker from the Miami area. The TOD was between nine and nine-thirty that evening, which meant they'd recovered the body only half an hour or so after the killer had left the scene.

She'd been found at Little River Park by a couple of kids on skateboards who reeked of cheap beer, pot and fear. They'd seen nothing of the murderer, but one of them had recognized the lady from her gleaming billboards, with the number plate on her Mercedes confirming the I.D. Like the others, she'd died from strangulation, without putting up any apparent fight.

Monica pulled a new, purple textbook from her draw and frowned at the yellow and pink ones that remained. Would she have to use them too, or would the new lead she'd discovered that evening ensure Faye was the last victim? The lead tip of her pencil raced through the blank pages, filling in all the details Pepe had been able to share. Monica didn't need to visit Faye's house to know what she'd find there, same as she had found in the first three homes. There was one thing connecting these women, and she'd bet her life that Faye was also a member of their small, apparently innocent club.

But even as she picked up the phone to call Pepe, one thought lurked at the back of her mind that had nothing to do with leads, and everything to do with an inexplicable sense of foreboding.

Where was her husband?

# CHAPTER FORTY-ONE

*Focus.*

After discussing some additional details about the latest murder, and validating Monica's suspicion about Faye, Pepe had also confirmed that Jeremy was not at the precinct. Upon hanging up she began to dial her husband's number, but then she paused and texted instead. Halfway through her message she stopped and deleted the message, putting her phone down and staring at it until the screen went dark. She needed to speak to him, but she couldn't. And she didn't know why.

*Focus.*

She kept forcing herself back to her search, back to her notebooks and the internet.

She flipped through the pages, entering in information from time to time from the pages she discovered. As each page turned, as each site was bookmarked and saved, a pattern began to emerge. She's been right. The women were all linked, and as Grady came and placed his head on her lap, she looked down at him and wondered at the workings of the universe. Had he been placed in her life, just for this one extraordinary moment?

Hannah Gallaway

Daleena Mendez

Debra Wright

Faye Bowman

They were all there, albeit on different sites, and then she did a combined search and found the site that contained them all.

When the full realization of her discovery hit, she was overwhelmed by opposing emotions battling inside her, and jumped up from her chair to run onto the patio. Her chest convulsed, taking huge lungfuls of the cool ocean air, even as the tears wracked her body and forced it back out. With a strange sense of detachment she noticed that her forearms were crushing her begonias, but none of that mattered anymore. She cried hard.

After several minutes she sensed the warm, furry body waiting patiently at her side. Poor Grady, even a dog could sense just how much had changed in their lives in such a short time. She dropped to her knees and a large, wet tongue licked at her cheeks, as if hoping to remove any evidence of her tears. Then, like a sliver of light through a cracked door, her hiccupping turned to a slight giggle, that graduated into a full, joyous laugh.

They would catch the bastard, now. And it was all thanks to Grady.

Monica finally gave up trying to block Grady from licking her face, grasping his snout and covering it in kisses. She let herself feel this adrenaline rush inside her, riding it like a new ride at the fair, her hands lifted from the safety bar.

"Grady, God gave you to me for so many good reasons!"

She almost started crying once more, Grady looking up at her with eyes that shone as if he knew what she was saying.

"I love you boy."

Monica jumped up from the deck and went back to the kitchen nook. She was refreshed and bursting with energy, settling back into her chair with more confidence than she had felt in her entire life. At the top of her browser the web address glared back at her, an open door to a world she was afraid of entering, and yet couldn't wait to leap into.

*www.elperroperdido.com*

"Lost Dog, you can run but you can't hide," she whispered.


Earlier that evening Monica had been walking through the apartment of Debra Wright when she noticed something considered average in any home, so when she saw it, she thought little of it.

A dog bowl.

Or two, to be precise. They were very similar to the ones she had in her utility room, one for food and one for water. Every second home had them, and that had to be the reason they'd been overlooked. After they had finished going through the three victims' residences, Monica asked Pepe if he'd noticed them.

"Dog bowls?" He paused, shrugging. "Sure, I noticed them. Why?"

Monica remained quiet, thinking. As if reading her doubt, Pepe followed with, "Almost every house in this area has a dog."

"Yes, but where are the dogs, Pepe?"

"With relatives, boarding in kennels, at the pound…I dunno. Wherever orphaned pets go."

Monica felt a slight wave of disappointment, but it was stifled by conviction.

"When you guys look after Grady for us we give you his bowls, his food, his harness, chew toys and…"

"Yeah, yeah. That dog has more trinkets than a newborn. What's your point?"

"All those items were still in the houses. It was as if the owner, *and the dog,* had just disappeared."

"Ok…"

"Which makes me wonder, if the dogs are gone, then why haven't the relatives asked about their whereabouts? And the only reason I can come up with to answer that is-"

"That the dogs were already missing," answered Pepe, glancing at her as the idea started to sink in. A slow grin spreading across his face. "I'll make some calls, but you may be onto something, Mamita…You may be on to something big."

# CHAPTER FORTY-TWO

Shelly was accustomed to being woken by Pepe's phone at all hours of the night, but didn't mind a bit. Her husband would fumble in an effort to silence it like a bomb about to go off, then turn to her in a panic to see if she'd been woken up. Shelly was always sure to lie still and keep her breathing deep and even. On this particular morning however there was no fumbling, or need to fake her slumber, as the handset continued to bounce along the nightstand unabated. Pepe was not in bed.

Shelly liked being Mrs. Pepe Torentez. From the day they had married they'd never spent a night apart, unless Pepe pulled an all-nighter on a case, or when he'd had to pull the midnight shift in his uniform days.

Growing up in California in the neighborhood she did, the only Latin people she had come across were those who cleaned the pools, did the landscaping, cooked meals and cleaned the houses. Then she'd met Monica, Latin in looks if not culture. She loved her dear friend, but it wasn't until she was introduced to Pepe that she understood the full depth and breadth of what it meant to be Latino. In many ways she was one, despite her blonde hair and blue eyes. In the end the culture wasn't an accent or a skin color, but a lifestyle, and one that had come so naturally to her.

"*Pepe!*" she called out, bleary eyed and half asleep. She knew he would be on his computer, just outside the bedroom door.

"Pepe, your phone, *dares prisa!*"

She was now on her elbows and knees, crawling across the spongy mattress with one hand pulling her long blonde hair out of her face, the other reaching out to grab the nuisance. The moment she made contact she felt the life go out of it. *Too late.*

"Baby?"

No answer. Ever since she'd run into his arms, clutching the small pregnancy stick with its thin red line, Pepe had been even more attentive than usual, almost *too* attentive. This morning however, he was clearly otherwise occupied and Shelly suddenly felt abandoned. She rolled herself out off of Pepe's side, still holding his phone in her hand as she walked zombie-like towards the kitchen, her feet dragging along the hardwood floor.

Reaching the door, she used the doorjamb to prop herself up as her eyes went to Pepe at the desk nearby.

"Honey?" she said, rubbing at her eyes. "What are you doing?" She held the phone out only to realize that when he responded, he was talking to someone else, her own cell wedged between his shoulder and ear as his clicked across the keyboard. Pepe would use Shelly's phone when he didn't want the caller to recognize his number, or the prefixes that were common to all detectives in Miami-Dade County.

She laid the handset beside his mouse, kissed him on the back of his neck, and continued to the kitchen in search of decaf coffee; something she was trying to get use too. A fresh pot was waiting for her, beside it a large mug.

In the six years they'd been married, Shelly had discovered that in addition to a terrible taste in movies, her tough, detective husband had a penchant for novelty coffee mugs. Three entire kitchen cupboards were crammed full of them, as well as about fifteen boxes upstairs in the attic. Their collection now numbered close to two hundred.

The cup this morning was white with a red unicorn, its legs galloping through the air. On its back rode a Cupid, his bow and arrow firing at a series of little hearts above his head, the unicorn below spearing one with his horn. Shelly smiled. Only Pepe would remember that their anniversary was a few days away, in the midst of hunting down a serial killer.

She poured her coffee into the Cupid cup and leaned her hips on the kitchen bench, crossing one foot behind her other ankle. Bringing the cup to her lips she didn't drink, but let the aroma wake her up as watched her husband work.

Pepe's phone began to vibrate once again, the name of a well known local journalist flashing across the screen. Clearly the media had found out about the latest murder, before they'd had a chance to announce it.

He hit cancel and focused on the voice in his right ear. It was confident and to the point.

"...that I cannot tell you, at least not right now. But what I can tell you is the name of the server. But even that will take me a while."

Pepe sat back in his office chair, placing his free hand behind his head and rubbing his neck in frustration. "Come on Jorge! It's a damn lost dog site. It's for people who actually *want* to be found!"

He leaned forward and propped his elbows atop his knees, the chair springs squeaking in protest. Jorge was the brother-in-law of one of Pepe's cousins, as well as a student at the local community college. The man was gifted. Gifted in the world of hacking into computers.

Pepe had called in a favor or two to helping smooth over some allegations of online security breaches and identity theft that might have ended up with Jorge copping some jail time, only months after the birth of his first child. From time to time, Pepe called Jorge to return the favor. The problem was, three high profile cases later, Jorge had paid his dues and knew it. Still, Pepe wasn't above reminding him of what he might have suffered.

"Jorge, your ass could be sittin' in the pen right now. *Nunca se sabe mi amigo!*"

"*You never know?*" Jorge laughed. "Oh I know. I know that the likeliest way I'll end up there is if I keep pulling this shit for you."

"Think of your daughter's first steps, her first word. Think of all the moments you've shared together."

"Shut up Pepe."

"Imagine if the first time she said 'Da-da' was in the visitation room."

Jorge groaned. "Aw-ite, aw-ite. Send me the name of the website and whatever you need to know," Jorge conceded.

"I can't email anything over. Got a pen?"

"Si."

He passed on the name of Monica's website, as well as the names of the victims and their email addresses, then closed Shelly's cell phone with a satisfied little snap. Of course they had their own IT guys that could do this work, and the FBI was itching to get involved, but those resources came wrapped in red tape. Every second counted, especially now that the murders were taking place more frequently. At first they'd thought the murders were only occurring on the first Sunday of every month, but there had only been ten days between the last two victims.

He gave a quick glance Shelly's way, flashed his 'Sorry I'm so busy' smile said, "*Buenos dias bella.*"

He didn't give his wife a moment to reply, before quickly turning back to the computer monitor.

> *Pepepossum: Should know more about the ip address tonight. Great work, Mamita!*

His cell started ringing again, the calls coming faster now, but as he picked it up a web message came from Monica, so he hit the silent button and popped it down once more.

*Gradysmom: I can't stop thinking about those women. We've got to get this guy.*

He began to reply, but another message appeared before he could hit enter. The woman could type.

*Gradysmom: I have never ID'd a killer before. It feels so personal. Should it feel personal?*

*Pepepossum: It's not personal, there are good guys and bad guys, but you can't let them get inside your head…Have you told J yet?*

*Gradysmom: No.*

*Pepepossum: Tell him.*

Now there was a pause, until finally the little icon that indicated she was typing popped up. A moment later, words followed.

*Gradysmom: He never came home last night.*

Pepe's heart sank. If Jeremy was off working cases, he didn't have anything to show for it. He hadn't presented any new leads or witnesses; he couldn't even be bothered answering Pepe's calls to account for his actions at all.

There was no viable explanation; this was the biggest case either of them had ever faced. Jeremy was a good cop, friend and husband, but he had issues and they all knew it. It was only a matter of time before he cracked, if he hadn't already.

This time when Pepe's phone went off, he was happy to answer it.

*Pepepossum: Phone call…ttyl.*

*Gradysmom: OK. Call me when you hear back from IT guy.*

"Torrentez," Pepe said, placing the phone to his ear.

"Where in the wide world of hell are you?" It was Chief Dorsey, and he was screaming.

"Get your Mexican, Puerto Rican, Cuban ass down here, Pepe. The latest vic is one of Miami's darlings, and all shit is hitting the fan. The Feds are breathing down my neck."

Pepe tried to explain the new online leads, the work that had to be done, but he was cut off before he'd finished saying "Chief".

"And where is that damn sharpshooter partner of yours? I thought you wanted to nail this case!" After a fiery series of words and curses the line went dead, and for a moment Pepe could do little more than stare at the screen in his hand, the sleepless night fast catching up with him.

His wife put a cup of caffeinated coffee—made just for him—beside the laptop, and gave him a light squeeze of the shoulder. Shelly never knew what to say when someone was murdered.

"Another one?"

"Last night," Pepe replied, his head sinking into his hands.

She lifted his face back up and pushed his shoulders back, straightening out his tie and adjusting his collar just the way he liked.

"Jeremy still missing?"

He smiled a bit, knowing better than to answer her. When Shelly had first suggested he might be having an affair, or a mental breakdown, Pepe had laughed. But he was a detective after all, and sometimes you just had to face facts. Of course, that didn't mean you had to share them.

"Dorsey said he's down at the station."

# CHAPTER FORTY-THREE

Pepe dropped by the precinct, planning to pick up some files before rolling out to Little River Park to visit the latest crime scene. He had only been down at headquarters for ten minutes when Chief Dorsey strode in his office.

"Don't start in on me chief, I'm on my way now. You coming too?"

Dorsey frowned. "Some of us have already been down there, Pepe."

Pepe picked up his duffle bag, stuffing a pair of footies inside, plastic covers that went over his own shoes to keep the crime scene clean. The bag also contained flashlights, batteries, latex gloves, Ziploc bags, envelopes, tape and a video camera.

"Sure, but I've been doing good work, Chief."

Pepe knew that Dorsey was an advocate of his, said he was a good cop and an above-average detective. He'd even downed a few too many whiskeys one night and slurred that he wanted Pepe to fill his shoes the day he was ready to step down. Truth be known, with all the pressure of cases like this one, that time might be right around the corner.

Pepe closed the blinds, smiling at the new set he'd recently had installed, not yet sabotaged by his partner.

Aware that he had broken just about every rule in the book by involving Monica in the investigation, he proceeded to delicately introduce the details of her discovery.

"Dammit Pepe, stop beating around the bush. There's a murderer out there somewhere."

"Okay, Chief," he said, raising his palms and proceeding to reveal the full extent of Jeremy's wife's research, and how she'd come up with a common link between the four victims.

"And I will bet you any amount of money this fourth vic recently lost a dog, and posted an ad on elperroperdido.com!"

Dorsey blinked, looking as shocked as Pepe no doubt had when Monica first shared her suspicions, and the logic of it all clicked into place.

"Damn, son," he said finally. "Who have you told about this?"

"I haven't told anyone. Monica only told me about it last night. I have a, uh…private contact working on the IP addresses and IDs on the site."

"You don't want our guys on it? Surely we should do at least one thing by the book on this investigation."

Pepe waved the words away. "You said it yourself boss, there's a murderer running around out there. You want the red tape and warrant requests? Or worse, the risk it's all over CNN by three o'clock?"

Dorsey nodded.

"This guy owes me a few hacks, you could say. He knows nothing but the fact I need the IP address for the user, or users, answering the ads posted by the four vics. Once we—"

Chief Dorsey stopped him right there. "I don't want to hear this. I don't want to know how you get what you get. At this point, I don't give an alligator's ass how you catch this guy."

Dorsey stood up from his chair, placing both hands in his pant pockets and looking out the window at the rows of men sitting at their desks. He had his back turned to Pepe as he spoke.

"Pepe, this is good, really good. And you say Monica Harlan came up with this?"

"Uh huh."

Dorsey continued watching the men, refusing to turn around. "Pepe?" He spoke his name in the form of a question, as if waiting to hear an answer.

"Yes?"

"Where is Jeremy?"

There was only a brief silence in that little room, but like rising floodwaters it seemed to come up from the floor and hit the ceiling, drowning them both.

Pepe decided to be straightforward, answering in the same calm tone Dorsey had used.

"Honestly Chief, I don't know."

"Do you know that Harlan has been down at the coroner's office pretty much every single day for the past couple of months? Are you aware he has been to each crime scene at least eight or ten times apiece?"

No, he hadn't known, because his partner hadn't contacted him about a single detail regarding the case. He hadn't contacted him at all.

"No Chief, I didn't know."

"Hmph," the older man grunted in frustration. "The men say he hasn't played any role in the case so far, as if refusing to share the evidence he finds."

Pepe prickled at this disloyalty, but kept his mouth shut.

That didn't stop the chief from turning to him, his deep brown eyes focused on him intensely.

"Odd, wouldn't you say?"

# CHAPTER FORTY-FOUR

As he drove down the 95, Pepe was still reeling from the conversation he'd just left. The chief had drilled him on keeping the new information quiet, to protect it from reaching the media. He was to coach Monica to do the same. What he hadn't understood, however, was why the chief didn't want him to share the new leads with his partner.

Pepe did not like the feeling in his stomach, nor the sweat on his forehead and the heat rising beneath his collar and tie. He felt as though it was hard to get a decent breath. Jeremy was one of the lead detectives on this case, and the only reason the chief might want to keep such important information from him was so ludicrous he could barely even think it aloud. Did he consider Jeremy as a media leak, or worse, person of interest in the killings?

Pepe shook his head. Jeremy might have been acting strange, obsessive even, but the chief knew that he was one of the good guys. Didn't he? Wasn't he? He hated himself for allowing the unwanted thoughts, but then Dorsey's revelation was hard to ignore.

With a light flush of embarrassment, Dorsey had admitted that each of his officers was being tracked via their mobile phones, himself and Jeremy included. He'd excused it as a security measure, but they both knew it was part of his war against corruption. Right now there were cops visiting businesses and gang headquarters on a regular basis, too regular, and one by one internal affairs planned to take them down from the inside out. The chief had taken a risk in telling him about the measure at all, but had clearly thought it worth the risk. According to Dorsey, the phone tracking had revealed an unusual occurrence.

Jeremy had been to the first two crime scenes up to eight times, before he and Pepe had even been assigned to the case.

"He's motivated," Pepe had said. "He's wanted to get this guy from day one."

"There's more to this Pepe."

Pepe had looked at his superior in shock. "What are you trying to say?"

Dorsey'd had the grace to look shamed by his words, but he'd spat them out nonetheless. "What if he knows the guy? What if he's trying to cover something up?" And even though he didn't believe it, or want to say it…what if it were him?

As Pepe turned his car onto Twenty-fourth Avenue his phone chimed, alerting him to a new text. Freeing it from the holder clipped to his belt he lifted it up and felt a wave of panic upon seeing his partner's name. *Get a grip, Pepe. It's your best friend.*

He picked it up and stared at the small blue screen.

*Are you coming?* it read. *I'm waiting for you.*

# CHAPTER FORTY-FIVE

Pepe stopped his car behind a police cruiser, put it in park, and then pushed himself out into the bright, breezy morning.

Within seconds he'd spotted Jeremy's tall form, drifting around the edge of the crime scene. He had so many thoughts running through his head, and so many questions he wanted to ask his partner. He made it a point to walk directly towards him, looking straight into his eyes as he approached. Confidence, not fear.

The cool blue gaze was hidden behind a pair of aviator's, and Pepe longed to snatch them off his face.

"What's wrong with you?" Jeremy asked calmly.

Pepe felt the blood drain from his face, and shrugged, walking right past Jeremy as if to look past the police tape.

"What do you think is wrong with me, *socio?*" Jeremy's silence made Pepe curl his fists in frustration. "Where the hell have you been, anyway? It's been two days since you last spoke to me, and Monica says you haven't been coming home at night."

As soon as the words left his mouth he realized his mistake, Jeremy's jaw hardening in an instant, but instead of trying to placate him he decided to go on the offensive.

"I get yelled at today by 'Hey, hey, hey!'" Pepe said, doing his best *Fat Albert* impersonation, "while the whole precinct wonders where my partner's disappeared to, and why he's acting so damn weird." He almost added, *while your wife's solving your cases for you*, but stopped himself.

Jeremy stood, arms crossed, refusing to join the conversation.

Pepe raised his hands in exasperation. "And you're asking me what is wrong with *me*? *Híjole*! I should be asking you what's wrong with *you*!"

"Pepe, shut up for a second," his partner said. "I've got a lead, but you've got to trust me on this."

"What lead?"

Jeremy looked down, grinding the heel of his boot into the dust. "I can't say."

"Why not?"

"Because…" He looked up for a moment, then away again. "You just have to have a little faith on this one." He put his large hand on Pepe's shoulder and squeezed. "Right, partner?"

"No Jeremy. Enough already."

He shrugged the hand off and turned around, walking away from Jeremy as fast as he could. He felt like he had survived some kind of mind game, giving Jeremy a piece of his frustration without revealing the full extent of the suspicions piling up around him.

Pepe crossed under the yellow tape. Once on the inside, the officers who'd answered the call the previous night walked up to greet him.

Pepe was listening to the officer and taking down the details of the boys who'd made the discovery, but the entire time he was aware of Jeremy's presence. He was watching him, he was sure of it. Eventually, unable to bear the sensation any longer, he turned and caught Jeremy's gaze swinging away, towards the trees. Pepe stopped the officer in mid-sentence, nodding towards his partner.

"Has he been here long?"

The officer had no idea who Pepe was talking about, and went on to describe the position of the body, which had since been removed.

Pepe had a strange feeling. Little nerves twitched on the back of his neck and the breeze blowing around him seemed to intensify each one, magnifying the sensation of a deer, walking into the crosshairs. As the wind raised the bumps on his skin, Pepe felt a chill. No, it was more than a chill—it was cold. He felt absolutely freezing in the extreme Miami heat.

As a little boy, Pepe had lived in a very small community north of Miami. Several people raised him, some of them family, others strangers. But all were Hispanic. They didn't have a television in his house, but there were plenty of people. For entertainment, the older kids would tell stories to Pepe and his sisters. This always occurred late at night, with a candle they had "borrowed" from the Catholic church down the block.

Lights switched off, they would place the candle in the middle of the floor and the children would sit in a loose circle, staring into the flickering flame. Then, just as the room had become eerily silent, one of them would say, "Can you feel it?"

This was followed by a pause that went for what seemed like the longest time. Pepe remembered the first time he'd taken a seat at the circle. He hadn't known what he was supposed to be 'feeling' when the question was asked. So he waited, the only obvious sensation was of his palms growing moist, and clasped tightly by the two youths sitting on either side of him.

They continued, "Can you feel it? Can you feel the *evil?*"

That word was spoken with a sinister inflection, one that Boris Karloff or Vincent Price would have been very proud of.

"There is evil in this house. There is evil in this room. There is evil in this circle."

Pepe had felt the sweat from his own hands mingling with the sweat of hands he now longed to let go of. He remembered wanting to get up and run. He remembered thinking, what if the evil in the room was in one of the people sitting next to him, and he was holding on to it?

"This evil, it might be across from you, or inside of you; it might be in all of us! Only one thing is for sure…it is very near you. Can you feel it?"

The game was meant to end when someone looked into the candle and made it go out. That person would be the one with the evil inside, but no one ever knew exactly who'd done it, the few times it had worked, or if an open window had done the job. Most of the time the game never made it past someone breaking the circle, and running off crying.

Now, a fully grown man who should have known better, Pepe was just like his five year old self, sitting in his apartment and shivering from evil. He rubbed his hands together in an attempt to dry his palms.

*Was it next to him? Across from him?*

The one thing he knew for certain was that it was near. That, or he was starting to lose his mind.

# CHAPTER FORTY-SIX

Monica tried to keep herself busy, cleaning the kitchen, picking up Grady's bowl and filling it with fresh water. For a little while the distraction worked, but as she wiped clean the counter top for the tenth time she realized she was nervous, very nervous. She threw the rag in the sink and walked over to the sliding glass door leading to the patio. Grady followed close behind, hoping for another jog on the beach. But Monica stopped at the doorway, her bare feet straddling the track.

She raised her hands, capturing her long hair as the wind tossed it in front of her face. Pulling it back behind her head, she wound it into a makeshift bun and walked over to her gardening stool, bun held in hand as she searched through a box of gardening odds and ends, trying to find something to hold it—a rubber band, pencil, anything. She was unsuccessful, and let it flop down again. Within seconds it was tangled back across her face.

The phone buzzed in her pocket, and she wrenched it out only to find that it was a message from Shelly, wanting to see if she was free to meet for lunch. Monica huffed, and felt guilty for being such a bad friend. Shelly had important news to share, and Monica had a feeling it might have to do with the pitter patter of little feet.

She let her thumb find the last text that Jeremy had sent. It was from days ago. Monica had been so wrapped up in the case that she'd somehow missed the fact her marriage had fallen apart. Jeremy had just disappeared, and the truth was she had pushed him away. He'd needed her support, first shooting those gang members, then taking on the biggest case in his life, and she'd made it impossible for him to come home at night without being interrogated.

Bad friend, bad wife.

And yet, she'd only wanted to help. She'd only wanted to join his team and become a bigger part of his life. Someone more than just the person he ate with, and slept with. He was the one who'd made it impossible, not her. He was the one who was always hiding something.

Monica felt something cold and wet behind her knee, and though she had felt the sensation a million times before, it always managed to be a surprise. She turned to see Grady wagging his tail and looking up at her.

"I love you, Grady boy," she said, cupping his snout in her hands.

The dog was wagging himself into a self-induced body slam, then *flop*! He hit the ground and rolled over onto his back, tail still wagging. Monica sat down next to him, not caring about her shorts getting wet. She rubbed Grady's belly, losing herself in the pleasure of his ecstasy.

It was easy to imagine how these women would take risks to reclaim their four legged loved ones. This guy, whoever he was, took advantage of a dog lover's devotion. He was smart, and very manipulative.

She tried to let herself think like him, and began to see how he would have to be very, very confident. He would maintain the upper hand across the board, catching the owner of the pet totally caught off guard. Instead of the usual suspicion inherent in strangers, he would be seen as a helper, a good Samaritan, riding the wave of happiness from his initial email, communicating the good news.

All the women had offered rewards. The amounts ranged from $500 to $2,500, and promised that the women were desperate enough to meet anywhere, and do just about anything. He picked public places, making his targets feel that he was a good guy, safety conscious and with nothing to hide. It was only when they got there they discovered that at night, the locations were quiet, dark, and desolate.

Monica wrote down everything she could dream about how the killer might lure these women. After writing several pages, she realized that he really had to do very little. It was as simple as searching the site and sending an email. Almost like a dating service.

She wished that Pepe would hurry with the information regarding the IP address, and hoped his hacker friend could access copies of the e-mails the killer had sent to the victims. Part of her feared that the IP would simply lead to a public computer somewhere, that it might be months before the actually get a positive ID. Then they still had to locate and catch the guy.

She paused, putting her pen down.

The biggest question was, why? Why was this guy killing all these women? It made no sense, at least not to her. Monica had never really dealt with criminals of this kind, few of the detectives at the precinct had. She had read lots of books in law school about serial killers and those who seemed to have the propensity to murder. But most of those seemed to have something to do with sex or power, or what some doctors wrote off as sheer insanity.

Their killer had no apparent sexual interest in these victims, and they hadn't been tortured in any way. It was as if he'd put them down in an act of mercy. Why?

Because they'd lost a dog? He deemed them irresponsible? He was a cat person? Maybe he'd just found a clever way to source victims who were easy targets. Knees pulled up to her chin and heels resting on the front edge of her chair, Monica glared at the yellow banner at the top of the website. *EL PERRO PERDIDO*.

It had to mean something more…it just had to. And after a while, it did.

# CHAPTER FORTY-SEVEN

*Find Your Lost Dog.*

Monica stared at the button, daring herself to click it.

She was on the edge of her seat and could feel her heart beating fast. It was crazy to mess with the investigation so directly. If Pepe wanted her to bait the killer, he would have suggested it. In fact, they would want to control the communication themselves. She could unwittingly give something away, let him know they were on his trail and send him off into hiding.

*And yet…*

It was her lead! She had brought the pieces together, so it felt fair that she get the chance to assemble them on the board.

Her hand hovered above the mouse as her eyes remained fixed on the small, green button. *Click it.*

She clicked it.

Monica did not stop and think too much about the names she should use or a strategic address, she simply imagined she was one of the victims, looking at Grady and conjuring the full vulnerability of losing him.

He was stretched out on the kitchen floor with his head facing away, but somehow he maintained an uncanny ability to know when she was looking at him. Maybe it was the silence of her fingers, stilled above their keys, or maybe, as Monica liked to believe, Grady just knew her.

She had not been staring at him for more than five seconds when *thump, thump, thump.* The tail started wagging slowly.

Monica smiled. *What would I do if I lost you boy?*

She knew better than to say this out loud and launch Grady to his feet, but she let herself stare at him for a while longer. It seemed to help her get in the mindset of someone desperate to find their baby.

She turned her full attention back to the computer monitor. Panic, depression, anxiety; the emotions rolled though her shoulders and flowed out her fingertips. As she clicked away Grady's tail stopped wagging. She couldn't help but smile once more.

*Carrie* was a girl she'd jogged with back in her college days. The last name she chose was *Powell,* from one of the librarians back in California.

Slightly harder was coming up with a name for the dog Carrie supposedly loved, but could not find. Her forefinger went to her lip as she tapped her nail against her front tooth. First she looked around the kitchen, but nothing struck her as being just right. A deep azure bowl caught her eye. Blue? Too masculine. Lou or…*Lulu*? That worked.

The rest seemed to flow with more ease as she continued to hit the tab key to move from box to box. Monica spent the next hour creating a fresh email account, verifying the account, and filling out the remainder of details elperroperdido.com required.

Next the site asked for a photo of the lost pet. Monica looked over at Grady again and considered the hundreds of photos conveniently sitting on her hard drive, but something told her not to use them. So far the murderer had targeted women with smaller dogs, and Grady had a distinctive white mask. If the killer happened to be someone they knew…That thought was ridiculous, and yet somehow it seemed like an unnecessary risk.

Instead she searched google for photos and soon found a female fox terrier that was red and brown. Lulu was born. She saved a copy of the photo to her desktop and uploaded the image to her account.

In one of the final steps, the site asked if she wished to advertise a reward. The victims had offered up to $2,500. Monica again sat and thought. Even if the murders weren't robberies, the rewards still hinted at the desperation, if not the affluence, of the owner.

Entering $2,500, Monica clicked the 'Continue' button, and was done. A moment later a confirmation email appeared in her new email account, thanking her for joining and wishing her good luck in finding her pet.

Monica clicked the link to sign in, nervously typing her false name and the password she'd just created. She hit enter, and a moment later Lulu's scruffy face appeared.

Monica wasn't scared, she was terrified.

Just an hour earlier she'd been Monica, a detective's wife with a dog named Grady. And now? She was Carrie Powell the owner of Lulu; a woman who hid things from her husband and courted serial killers.

Her skin crawled.

The monitor cast its cool blue light across her face, and she was struck with the sense that someone was looking right at her, a monster invited into her home. She glanced at the small computer camera at the top of the screen and stopped herself from covering it. There was no need to be silly. But was the killer was scrolling through the listings right now? He might be reading her ad at that very moment, in a room, in a house somewhere. She felt in her bones that he was close, watching her at that very moment.

"Hey."

Monica jumped three feet out of her chair and collapsed sideways, shrieking like a banshee. Grady jumped up, barking in confusion.

Jeremy commanded him to be quiet and he obeyed, trotting over to welcome his master home.

"I'm sorry I scared you," he murmured.

Monica gathered herself, slowly standing to her feet.

"My God Jeremy, where did you come from? I didn't hear the garage door."

"I saw the light and came in from the back thinking you might be with your flowers. What are you doing?" he asked, looking over her shoulder at the computer.

Monica found herself trying to block the screen with her body, not ready to tell Jeremy about the little trap she had just laid out. She was not happy with how things were between them; they hadn't talked in a long while.

For the first time in five years, she found herself telling her husband a lie.

"I was e-mailing...Alton." She continued talking, too afraid of the silence if she stopped. "He said he was coming to Miami soon to look over a location for some movie with Garth Brooks. 'A cowboy cop in Miami' or something. Cool, right?" She smiled, forcing herself to look him in the eye. "Gonna have a killer theme song."

She popped a bubble, knowing that she'd talked long enough. Jeremy didn't say a word, walking over to the refrigerator and gulping down some orange juice straight from the carton.

"There was another murder last night." Then, sarcastically, "Oh, that's right, I'm sure your partner already told you." He placed the carton back inside the fridge, shutting the door after doing so. "You know, baby…" Hands on the kitchen counter, he leaned towards her. "I don't like this at all. I don't like you doing whatever it is you're doing, and I don't like you getting close to things like this. I've tried for five years to keep you out of all this mess, and now you're right smack in the middle of it, and…" His hands clenched into fists as he raised his eyes to her. They were fathomless. "This will not end good for you." He paused, "This will not end good."

The words settled in the pit of Monica's stomach like acid as Jeremy turned toward the back door. She remained frozen, still guarding the computer screen.

Before he could leave she said, "What do you mean?"

He stood with his back to her, shoulders tensing as he found his own words. "You know I…care for you. I love you Monica. But there's a lot you don't know, things I've tried to protect you from. You're walking into something you don't understand, and if you're smart you'll know to leave it alone."

He turned to look at her one last time. "I won't be coming home until you quit this."

Moments later the door slammed closed and Monica was left standing in front of the computer, confused, alone and suddenly feeling nauseous.

# CHAPTER FORTY-EIGHT

Al placed his clipboard on the stainless steel bench, rustling the blue plastic sheet draped over the young woman's corpse.

"It's like I told Jeremy, time of death around 9:00P.M., give or take a quarter of an hour."

Pepe lowered his phone, his text half finished. "What did you say?"

"I said I put the T.O.D around 9:00P.M., from the best I can—"

"No, no, I mean about Jeremy."

The large, bristling, grey brows drew together.

"What about the guy?"

"You just said something about him."

"Pepe, I didn't say anything about Jeremy, I only said 'like I told Jeremy.' No big deal." He shook his head and went back to work studying the body. "What the hell's going on with you guys? It's like I'm walking on egg shells all the time."

Being a born interrogator, Pepe couldn't help but answer Al's question with one of his own.

"What makes you think there is something going on between *us* two?" Pepe tapped his chin. "You know I saw on Dr. Phil, when a person asks another person what's wrong, often the problem is really with themselves." He nodded, finding strength in the idea. "*Projection*, it's called. You projecting on me, Al?"

Al sunk into a chair, his heavy frame settling under the weight of the day. "Pepe, I haven't seen you and Harlan together in days, and when I mention the guy's name you almost jump out the window." He paused, as if trying to

153

read Pepe's expression. "Now maybe I'm 'projecting on you', but the fact is Jeremy is here every other second, pulling apart each piece of evidence. Asking me again and again about certain details, and how they might be interpreted—"

Pepe stopped him. "He's here all the time, huh?"

Al nodded. "I'm gonna start charging the guy rent. If you two are having a lover's quarrel, send the guy some damn flowers! I am sick of him, Pepe, looking over my shoulder with a thousand and one questions."

Al picked up one of the cool, inanimate hands and ran a Q-tip under the blueish nails.

"After the lead we got this morning, he hasn't been around. Ran straight out the door like he had the devil on his heels."

"Lead? What lead?"

Alan placed the hand back down and looked up, pale eyes widened.

"He didn't tell you about the Euthasol?"

Pepe shook his head and Al sat back against the bench, arms crossed over his chest. "What kind of damn investigation is this, Pepe—"

"What the hell is Etheesole?"

"*Euthasol.* This morning I discovered very fine needle punctures on the back of each victim's neck, in the hair line. Easy to miss. This led me to test for different sedatives, and I found minute traces of Euthasol. Not enough to have knocked them out, but would probably make them go limp or numb for twenty, thirty seconds or so. Explains the lack of struggle."

He paused for a moment and Pepe nodded, trying to keep the shock off of his face.

"I was going to call you but Jeremy stopped me, said he'd tell you him—"

"You get any new information, you come directly to me, okay?"

Al raised his hands in supplication. "Of course, Detective. And hey, I didn't get you guys in trouble by bitching at Dorsey about Jeremy being down there all the time, did I? Did he say something to you?"

Pepe saw this as a great exit strategy, and he ran with it. "Dorsey came barking at me all morning, and Jeremy too."

Al shrugged, but kept quiet.

"So next time you want to cause trouble for me and my partner, would you come to us first?" Al nodded, and Pepe decided to pile it on some more. "Me and Jay got our own way of doing things, Al, and it ain't always the same. This case ain't like any other case, *muchacho!*"

"I'm sorry, Detective Torentez."

Pepe stood a little straighter, reminding himself he'd likely be the new chief detective very soon.

"I didn't mean to cause you boys trouble." Al smiled, adding, "Next time I go to the chief, I might be coming to you, Pepe—I mean, Chief Torentez."

Pepe smiled, this time for real.

# CHAPTER FORTY-NINE

As Pepe walked out to his car he went to call Jeremy, ready to blast him for his apparent oversight in sharing a pivotal new piece of evidence. *What was the guy thinking?* But as his finger scrolled the contacts, he paused and decided to place another call instead.

"Hola Jorge, see you outside Wal-Mart in fifteen."

Before the computer hacker could reply with some bullshit excuse, Pepe hung up. Wal-Mart had become their regular meeting place, the perfect cover. Everyone had a reason to go there. Suits and Baggies.

Fifteen minutes later Pepe walked up to Jorge, sprawled across a plastic pool chair in the lawn and garden area. As soon as he saw Pepe he stood up and began to walk away, pausing by a pimply faced employee to say loudly, "Tell your customers to try that one." He pointed at a bright pink chair opposite the one he'd just vacated. "If I had the monies, I would pay for one just like it. Read me, amigo?"

The store clerk thanked him, shrugging and turning back to his shelf of garden gnomes, but Pepe caught his eye and nodded.

He walked over to the chair and sat down, slipping his hand under the cushion to discover a small, folded sheet of paper. A moment later it was tucked inside his coat pocket, his hand exploring the space once more to ensure he hadn't missed anything. The second pass revealed nothing, so he stood up and walked back to his car.

Once inside Pepe stretched the wrinkled paper across his steering wheel. He could tell at first glance there wasn't much to read, only a single Web address that was a jumble of irregular letters and numbers, scrawled across the corner. Underneath was a message.

*Need one, maybe two weeks, and I'll have your name. In the meantime, enjoy reading.*

That was all. Pepe put the car into gear and pulled out of the parking lot, turning north, towards an internet cafe about two blocks away. Once inside he selected a computer in the back corner, placing his credit card into the slot and typing the address Jorge had included. When he hit enter a new window popped up containing several e-mail files. Pepe couldn't help but glance at the people around him, not that it really mattered, but he realized that he was beginning to trust no one.

A line at the top instructed Pepe to refresh the page daily as new files and data came through. These included hundreds of responses to the lost dog ads; Jorge had no idea which ones Pepe might be interested in.

*When you narrow it down to certain messages, text me the screen name, and I will get to work on the ID. Shouldn't take more than ten days.*

Pepe tensed. They needed a lead now; in ten days' time they'd probably have another body on their hands. He began to scan through the messages, all polite in tone, without a single perverted sentence to give the murderer away. As he read he made a list of all the screen names, taking note of the ones that had responded to more than one of the victims. Then, *jackpot!*

Several users had replied to at least two of the victims, as the missing dogs had been similar and description and location, but there was only one screen name that had responded to all four women.

*Rescuegy.*

Again he glanced around, almost expecting the murderer to appear over his shoulder with a needle in hand. Or Jeremy, and that icy blue gaze. *"Got a lead, partner?"*

But there was no one, bar the usual assortment or bored kids, students and tourists.

Turning back to the screen his fingers trembled as he isolated the messages from rescuegy. Each one seemed to be almost identical, as if they'd been copied for the most part.

Sickeningly, the replies all mentioned the pain and anxiety suffered as the result of losing a loved one, and mentioned that *he*—Pepe's skin prickled—

had lost an animal once that he'd loved dearly. He understood their anguish, which is why he owned and operated a home-based rescue centre. In a final dose of irony, rescuegy said that he was 'pro-life', believing that no lost dog should ever have to be put down.

Pepe grimaced. *Tell that to the electric chair.*

Pepe opened up a new window and searched for *rescuegy*, but found nothing. Of course, that would have been too easy he thought to himself. Clicking out of each screen Pepe made sure to clear the history cache before turning the computer off, which he got yelled at for, but didn't care. Pepe had a lead…and a very bad feeling.

# CHAPTER FIFTY

Pepe and Monica were sitting in a corner booth at Arlo's, quiet as a couple on a very awkward blind date.

"You said you had something you wanted to tell me, Pepe?"

Pepe straightened his tie and then unfolded the napkin hastily, slinging it across his lap.

"You're lost dog lead has delivered, I've got something big."

Monica leaned forward in anticipation. "Really?" Then paused, thinking of her husband. "Where's Jeremy? Have you told him?"

Pepe looked away, a blush forming beneath his tan.

"Monica, I—"

"Hello, hello!"

Arlo's voice rolled across the room like thunder, and like accomplices caught red handed, they jumped in their seats. The restaurateur crossed the room, dishing out pleasantries as he moved his ample girth through the room in a beeline for their table. When he reached them he placed his palms on Monica's shoulders and gave her a quick kiss on each cheek, then took the napkin from the table, unfolded it, and draped it across her lap.

"And hello to you too, Señor Torentez! Shall I get another silverwares for Señor Jeremy and Señorita Shelly, hmm?"

Monica froze. Spending time together without Jeremy's knowledge or approval left them both uneasy, even as she reminded herself he'd left them no other option. Still, they could have chosen a less familiar place to meet.

"Jeremy is busy…" Pepe stuttered, "and Shelly…" His mouth hung open, slowly opening and closing as he struggled to think of how his wife might be occupied. If it weren't so awkward, Monica might have laughed. "Shelly is pregnant!" he finally spat out, only to snap his mouth shut in horror.

Now Monica was the one gaping, and Pepe's mouth—paralyzed only a moment ago—went into overdrive. "Well, she might be…she doesn't know—I think she is, but …." Eventually he shut up and dropped his head in his hands. "Oh my god, she's gonna cry when she hears I stole her big moment."

"Oh, Pepe, I am so happy for you!"

Monica was practically doing aerobics as she bounced atop her seat. But for all her excitement, Pepe seemed to be sinking even lower.

"But I won't say a word. I will save my screams for her later, when she tells me herself. I promise." She looked at Arlo with a serious face. "And you will too, Arlo, *right?*"

"Of course, of course, bella!" He clapped a meaty hand on Pepe's shoulder. "Congratulations, Papa!"

For all their reassurances, Pepe's face remained pale and drawn.

"Arlo, you can't say a word, not a word. *Tus comprende?*"

"I say this already, yes, did I not?"

Pepe shook his head, burying his face in his hands once more.

"What is it with you and Señor Jeremy?" he pouted. "So serious all the time! Always keeping secrets!" He glanced at Monica only to quickly look away. "I mean…" He began moving the salt and peppershakers on the table, slightly rearranging them. "Oh never mind." He waved his hand and began to move away, but Monica caught his arm.

"Don't worry Arlo, they're just under a little pressure at the moment. A little good news is all they need." As he wandered off, she turned to Pepe. "Have you told Jeremy yet?"

"No," he said, focusing very hard on the silverware before him.

Monica sighed. It seemed Pepe's relationship with Jeremy had grown just as strained as her own. But as much as she wanted to try to fix things, she knew she had to give the men some space to sort it out.

She also had to tell Pepe about the trap she'd set in the form of Lulu, her 'missing' terrier, but couldn't bring herself to formulate the words. She didn't have to be a mind-reader to know he wouldn't approve, but she didn't know if the news would be met with criticism, or out-right condemnation. Pepe wasn't acting like himself.

In the end, she simply blurted it out.

"I am Carrie Powell."

"Huh?"

"I am Carrie Powell, Pepe."

Pepe blinked at her, silent, and Monica realized that she must sound like a mad woman.

Taking a deep breath, she decided to get it all out as quickly as possible. "I placed an ad on elperroperdido.com. Don't be mad, I know it was probably a dumb thing to do," she blustered on, "and I know that you and Jeremy are going to yell at me, call me stupid and probably throw me off the case…" Monica launched into a long list of reasons and excuses, bargains and threats, until a few minutes later she realized she was rambling, and completely out of breath. She paused and saw that Pepe didn't look angry but…thoughtful. She steadied her breathing and began to more carefully out outline the details of what she'd done, the steps she'd taken, how she set up the fake e-mail account, the whole nine yards.

As she continued speaking he began to smile a bit, and with growing confidence she explained how much she wanted to bait the killer before he could claim another victim. But when he finally spoke he didn't ask her about her plan, or applaud her initiative. Instead he said, "Does Jeremy know about this?"

"No, I haven't told him, but I will—"

Pepe cut her off. "*No!* No…I mean, let's just keep this between us for right now."

Monica nodded, guessing he had come to the same conclusion she had: Jeremy would be furious to know she was potentially putting herself in the cross-hairs of the killer. Furious at *both* of them.

"We'll tell him when the time is right," she said.

Pepe nodded, looking distracted.

For a moment they sat in silence, both lost in thought, but eventually Monica looked up and smiled.

"Well, what do you think? Are we going to catch this lost dog killer?"

Pepe's deep brown eyes crinkled in amusement, or exhaustion. It was hard to tell. "We might. But for now, you did it, Monica."

"Did what?"

"You named the serial killer. That's a big deal you know. In the history books he'll be forever known as the Lost Dog Killer."

They smiled at each other, aware that every day brought them closer to catching the monster and locking him up for good. But then their smiles wavered, as if for some reason the very thought was too much to bear. The chance of the serial killer randomly selecting her was a thousand to one, and yet she felt targeted already.

Pepe and Monica spent the next hour and forty minutes formulating a plan that seemed brilliant and horrifying at once.

They were going to launch a sting.

When Monica first posted her ad, she'd hoped to lure the killer into contacting her and potentially revealing details about his (or her) identity. She had not, in a million years, imagined going out to meet him in a dark, lonely park. But Pepe assured her that if she were confronted, there would be unmarked cars nearby and officers lurking in every corner, and he would have full and open communication with Monica at all times via a wire.

Monica was thrilled with this escalation of her plans, but Pepe knew her safety had to be his number one concern. He'd considered putting a female officer in her place, but there was something about Monica that convinced him she had to be the one, quite aside from the fact she'd probably kill him herself if he didn't let her see this through.

"Are you going to tell Jeremy when you get back at the station?"

"No, let's wait until we see if we get a nibble on your e-mail first."

Her shoulders dropped a fraction, and Pepe couldn't tell if she was disappointed, or relieved.

"Okay, I'm going home to see if the fish are biting."

She stood up, digging in her purse for some cash to cover her drinks, but he waved her away.

"Work expense," he said.

She nodded. "Well, I'll let you know when anything comes through."

Monica looked excited, but afraid, and Pepe wondered if he wasn't making a monumental mistake by involving her as he was. Too late now. She leaned in kissed him on his cheek, congratulated him again about the baby, then walked away.

Pepe sat alone at the table, stewing. With the emails in his pocket and Monica setting a trap, the detective was sitting in the catbird seat, and yet for all the strings in his web, he couldn't help feeling hopelessly tangled himself.

He tried to iron out his thoughts, reminding himself that he wasn't the one on trial here. Pepe was simply doing his job, protecting people and applying justice. So why did he feel that every time they progressed the case, he was hammering another nail in his partner's coffin?

Jeremy wasn't the killer, he couldn't be—the thought was too...monstrous. But he was hiding something big, and it was related to the murdered women. Had he been in love with one of them perhaps? Pepe had been a detective for long enough to know his instinct was usually right, and his instinct told him that Jeremy's obsession and evasiveness went far beyond a zeal for the job, or personal eccentricity. He just hoped that when it all came to light, Jeremy's secrets wouldn't bury them all.

# CHAPTER FIFTY-ONE

For the past eleven months Ramos Salodimas had negotiated the deal of a lifetime—of his lifetime, for sure. He had managed the sale of his privately owned pier and all his property around it to a huge hotel chain from the United States. The deal still had another month or so of lawyers crossing the t's and dotting the i's and Ramos had not yet signed his name, but when he did it would free him from the monotony of the marina lifestyle, and leave a cool thirty-eight million dollars in his bank account.

When first approached with the offer he had tried to act as if he were expecting it. And maybe in some ways he had been. But still, when he heard the word *million*, he didn't care what number came in front of it, and he nearly passed out to learn that number was thirty-eight.

He'd left the meeting light on his feet and with a head full of plans. They had nothing to do with new clothes or fast cars, or staying where he was. Instead he wished to travel, and more specifically, to travel to wherever he might find his little girl. Ramos knew he wouldn't be happy until he had seen that she was happy… especially now that he had the means to ensure she never worked another day in her life.

It was that simple. But for all his newfound enthusiasm, a small voice haunted the back of his mind. Ramos had spent years observing the rich, the powerful, and the greedy…If there was one thing he knew, it was that money spelt trouble. And there was no way he was going to let trouble find its way to his little Pepita.

Ramos only knew the three men as Damario, Phoenix, and Ciro. And he knew that they worked for the notorious mobster, Emilio Ignacio.

He had leased yachts to the three thugs many, many times over the past decade. He didn't know exactly what they used them for, and didn't want to know, they simply picked them up, kept them in the harbor, and never once went out to sea. The leases were always for a few weeks at a time, and came with a single mandate: the boats had to be docked in the slips toward the end of the pier, as far away from anyone as they could get.

"We don't wanna bother no one with our parties."

Ramos was only too happy to comply with the request; from experience he'd learned it was good for business to place such people away from the conservative, law-abiding clientele anyway. However, he also knew these three were not holding the kind of parties that he was accustomed to.

It didn't take long for the pattern to become apparent. Boats pulled into dock late or very early in the morning, with no one saying a word on board. Generally Ramos would note ten or twelve passengers across the three vessels, Damario, Phoenix and Ciro captaining each, and disembarking with large coolers held in their arms. Ramos didn't need more than his sixth-grade education to know they weren't filled with beer and fish.

Their boss, Emilio Ignacio, was the current king of drug lords and was well known for smuggling huge quantities of drugs into the United States. He'd learned who the men were working for almost from the start, when Damario, Emilio's second in command, had looked up and down the marina and said, "Tu Cara will like this, he will like this very much."

Ramos had paled, and turned his face to hide his surprise. Everyone knew who the nickname 'Tu Cara' belonged to. It meant, "Your Face", but unlike Scarface, Emilio's face was unmarked. He didn't attract such a name for his own disfigurement, but for the many mutilated faces he'd left in his wake.

# CHAPTER FIFTY-TWO

Ramos had just returned from his lawyer's office, his steps light as air as he thought of the arrangements he'd made and the future rolling out before him. All the years of hard work, and all his lonely nights, were finally going to pay off.

He opened the door to his office and stepped through, holding it open with his right hip as he struggled to put down his briefcase and keys without spilling his coffee. In a few weeks, he would close the door to this room, and never set a foot inside it again. The thought made him smile.

The cold air from his air conditioner hit his face, and a split second later, so did a fist. Ramos was stunned as he fell back against the wall, the hot coffee splashing upon his chest and seeping through the fine white cotton to his tender skin below. Phoenix had not struck him hard enough to knock him out, but enough to show that he meant business.

Mission accomplished.

Ramos tried to focus, gathering his wits as he noted Damario, Phoenix and Ciro all stood around. A fourth man was seated, whom he had never seen before.

Ciro and Phoenix grabbed Ramos underneath his arms and carried him to the little couch to the side of his desk. They threw him down in the center of it. The stranger remained settled behind Ramos' desk.

"*Estes el hombre!* You are *the man*, but now you wish to be a rich man, too?"

Ramos blinked at the cold, dark eyes and knew without a doubt that he was sprawled before one of the most dangerous mobsters in the world. As if noting his sudden discomfit, Emilio Ignacio nodded.

"You know who I am. So, you know I have been a good customer to you for a long, long time. I'm sure that you can understand that when I heard our little arrangement was to come to an end, I was..." The eyes narrowed menacingly, "not happy."

He stood up from the desk and walked around to stand before Ramos. He was wearing white pants and a very pale yellow shirt, one that was made out of very soft cotton, almost translucent.

"Mr. Salodimas, I have come here requesting that you do not sell this pier to the hotel company. You see, this would not be good for my fishing expeditions, and because I am very..." he slowly clenched and unclenched his fists, "*very*, passionate about fishing, it would not be good for your health, either. The people here respect me, they respect my wishes, and it is my wish that things here remain as they are."

Ramos was well aware of the situation, even without ever speaking to the men about what they did. It was clear that Emilio was keeping the drugs hidden on the docked boats. He would send the original boats out to channel the waters as decoys to attract the authorities. The U.S. Coast Guard knew the name and the registration number to each of his boats, and while they were being boarded and searched, the drugs were loaded onto three other vessels leased from elsewhere. Ramos had seen them hovering outside the berths, likely belonging to some rich American Emilio had bribed—or left marked with his knife.

"Our arrangement is good here, Ramos. I don't wish to buy the pier from you at thirty-eight million dollars, or even half that. No, that is way too much money. And if I paid you anything at all, then the U.S. customs would suspect something, yes? So it is best to just leave things the way they are, no?"

It was Ramos' turn to talk; Emilio wanted his answer.

If only Ramos knew what to tell him. Emotions were twisting and turning through his stomach and heart, the same feeling he had experienced the day he'd given Monica away and felt a part of him die inside. But things were different now, he had options, even if they appeared to be dangerous ones. Ramos would not give up his chance to find Monica, or provide for her. Nor was he going to work for a drug lord for the rest of his life.

He looked straight back into the eyes of Emilio Ignacio.

"I will not make this deal with you, Emilio. I don't want any trouble from you, but I am sure you can find another place to lease your boats."

The words fell out of his mouth in nervous little bursts, and he fought the desire to touch the cross and beads in his pants pocket.

Emilio looked at him serenely. "Ramos, you have always been a proud man, a very proud man. I know this. But I know that you will see things my way, sooner or later."

He lowered himself onto the couch besides Ramos and leaned close, as if to pat him on the shoulder. Ramos didn't see Ciro holding the knife until its rubber handle had been slipped into Emilio's palm. A moment later the tip was pointed at the small, soft spot below Ramos' left eye.

"*Tus Cara*. Do you know this is what they call me, Ramos?"

Ramos knew he did not have to answer the question, only that he was going to die, or be left wishing he had. Still, the sale would go ahead regardless, and the lawyers had been told about Monica. She would receive the money, even if he was not around to give it to her himself. A small sense of peace came upon him, even as his body was flooded with adrenalin.

"I don't want to cut you, Ramos. See, if I did, the locals would know that Tus Cara was doing business here, and I don't want everyone to know. So relax."

Ramos found little comfort in his words, determined as he was not to concede.

"I have a better way; Emilio Ignacio always has a better way. See, I know that things are going to stay the same around here. I know this in my heart because it is the heart that matters, no?"

Ramos gulped as Emilio's eyes flickered down to the large, brown coffee stain over his chest. Was he going to cut his heart right out of his chest?

"What we carry in our hearts, this is what makes us do what we do."

Emilio nodded, lowering the knife point and tapping it against the coffee sodden fabric.

"I am not going to cut you Señor Ramos, not with this knife anyway…But I will promise you one thing. If you sell to the Americans, I will kill your daughter."

Ramos's eyes forgot how to blink, how to breathe. Even his heart seemed to stop.

"Oh, I see this is a surprise to you."

Ramos shook his head, still trying to recover.

"I...I don't have a daughter, Emilio."

"It was news to me too, amigo. But I know you do, and if you do not obey me, I will cut her into little pieces and bring her to you in coolers. Then we can go fishing together, my friend, and with bait so sweet, I'm sure we'll catch Poseidon himself."

"I do not have a daughter!"

Emilio smiled at Ramos, almost sadly, before turning to Damario.

"Bring her in."

As Damario walked to the door Ramos' heart started beating so hard he thought it was going to burst out his chest. *How had they found her?* His baby, his little girl. As the love pored through him the fear quenched it just as quickly. To watch a single hair on her head harmed, and know that he had brought evil upon her, would kill him.

The door flew open, and Ramos strained to see around Damario's bulky figure. When he finally stepped to one side, pulling the woman roughly inside by the shoulder, Ramos was not met with the young, beautiful vision he had expected, but that of an old, broken prostitute. Track lines marked her arms, and her eyes were glassy. In an orange latex miniskirt, no bra, and plastic heels, Ramos wondered what his daughter had to do with a hooker. Then recognition struck, and he almost suffered his second heart attack in one day.

"Maricita!"

His wife, and Monica's mother. Except she wasn't that woman anymore. Not even close. For all the nights he'd spent alone and cursing her, his heart ached for her now. He had struggled, but she'd been ruined in every sense.

"That's right, Ramos. This is Maricita, your wife, or what is left of her. She looked better years ago, no? Back when I first found her strutting around the docks, with her tight little ass hanging out her shorts." He smiled. "Then she got to playing with the candy too much, and I had to turn her out. But she kept coming back, like they always do. I kept sending her away until one day she came back to me with an offer I couldn't refuse. You see, I knew I couldn't afford to buy you, and I knew you didn't have a taste for candy yourself. But darling Maricita here reminded me of that little angel I'd seen crawling all over the piers. Monica, I think it was?"

Ramos stiffened at the name, and Maricita glanced up at her husband, her empty eyes flickering with life. "I'm sorry, Ramos—" she began, only to stop as Emilio stood up and walked over to her. She dropped her head as he eased behind her, his hand cupping her cheek like a loving admirer.

"Sorry, my love? Why?"

She shook her head, mouth tightly shut.

Emilio glanced at Ramos from over her shoulder. "She's no longer the woman you knew. Only a junkie."

With that, he placed his free hand at her shoulder as his other fingers slipped to her chin, and with a sudden jerk her head snapped back; her neck along with it. Ramos cried out and staggered to his feet as the woman dropped to her knees and slumped onto the floor, dead.

"I did her a favor," said Emilio, dusting his hands on his pants and nodding at two of the men to clean up his mess. Ramos watched in a stupor as they wrapped his ex-wife in plastic, while Emilio continued speaking. "We will find your daughter, Ramos, and when we have her, you will know you need to play my way."

Ramos could only shake his head, caught in a deep, thick sense of shock.

As he walked out the door, Emilio spoke over his shoulder. "Women, huh?" He chuckled, as if they were two friends who'd met up after a hard day at the office. "Can't live with them, can't live without them."

# CHAPTER FIFTY-THREE

A white Lincoln was parked across the street, pointing downhill from the front entry gate to the Howard's sprawling home. Inside sat Damario, Phoenix and Ciro, debating the many potential excuses they could use to make it past the Howard's intercom. So far no unanimous agreement had been reached, and it was becoming clear that they would have to resort to drawing toothpicks. But just as Ciro broke one of the small timber splinters in half, Damario grunted, nodding at the gates ahead. A slick, black Lamborghini had purred past and was now waiting patiently as the large, iron barrier slid open.

Phoenix started the Lincoln, jerked it into gear and slammed the accelerator to the floor, racing across the street. The tires squealed as they burned across the tar, Pheonix cutting the wheel sharply to the left and bouncing through the gate, behind the Lamborghini. All the commotion had attracted Alton Howard's attention, sitting in his black convertible and peering over his shoulder in confusion.

He turned back to switch the car off, leaving it parked next to a large, multi-tiered fountain, before opening his door and getting out.

The three men piled out before he could reach them, all wearing suits and sunglasses. Howard looked wary, but kept a light smile on his face.

"Hello, gentlemen. May I help you with something?"

Damario usually did all the talking and so he began, while Ciro and Phoenix moved subtly around him, flanking Alton.

"Ju must be Señor Alton Howard?"

Alton stuck his right hand out to greet him, Damario taking his open palm and pulling his arm straight out, so that his elbow was locked in place. With his free hand, Damario grabbed underneath Alton's elbow and began pressing up in a violent jerking motion. The crack was audible, and a moment later Alton Howard was doubled over and crying out in pain as he gripped his arm against his body. As he fell to the ground he was swarmed by Ciro and Phoenix, who were armed with duct tape and a large white sock. The two men worked quickly, stuffing the sock in his mouth as he continued to groan, then sealing it in with a few twists of tape wrapped around his skull. Damario gave his orders with all the cool and calm of his boss.

"Put him in the garage and keep him alive, for now. We might need him later if the girl's not here."

They dropped him in the back corner of the garage, behind a perfectly restored 1932 Model A Ford, his wrists zip locked to the leg of a stainless steel set of shelves. The best way to maintain an element of surprise was by walking in through the backdoor of someone's home, and so they headed past the pool, taking only cursory notice of the guest houses, spa and putting green.

A sliding glass door at the back of the house was wide open, allowing for the afternoon breeze. It put them in the kitchen, but there was no one around. They drew weapons, three 9mm pistols with silencers, and spread out to search for their target.

After a quick survey of the ground floor, they met back at the bottom of the huge staircase in the foyer. It seemed the staff took the weekends off, and the Howard women were either out, or upstairs.

Damario led the way.

Earlier that day Alton had phoned Gloria to tell her he would be leaving for Miami to lock off the contracts for his latest movie. As he was taking the private jet, he'd asked if she wanted to go with him to see Monica.

Sitting at her makeup dresser as she took the call, Gloria stared into the angled mirrors and thought of how she had not seen Monica in over six years. There was no doubt in her mind that Monica would be gorgeous, more gorgeous than ever, and worse, her beauty would only serve to highlight Gloria's slump into middle age.

She could barely contain her spite. "I told you I don't ever want to see that ungrateful, Mexican, bitch *ever again!*"

With that, she'd hung up the phone and remained completely unaware that Alton had returned to grab a change of clothes and an overnight bag, before heading to the airport. She was also unaware that the next hour would be the last, and most horrifying one of her life.

Typically the three thugs did their job without thought or motive. They didn't ask questions or take any great pleasure in their work; they simply killed whoever they were told to. But once they'd spent an afternoon with Gloria Howard, they felt they were doing the world a very big favor indeed.

# CHAPTER FIFTY-FOUR

Detective Torentez had only used the Miami Dade County private plane on two other occasions, trips he'd taken with the chief for important presentations and conferences around the country. The seats were small and there was no way anyone could stand up, but what it lacked in luxury it made up for in speed. It sure beat a long, boring drive to Tampa.

As the propellers hummed outside the window, Pepe's mind reeled.

*What the hell was he doing?*

The clouds flashed by, his thoughts floating as if similarly detached from grounded reality. He just could not believe all of this was really happening.

"About fifteen minutes, sir."

Pepe nodded at the pilot and buried himself in his notebook to limit any further conversation. The pages were filled with information he'd received from Jorge, only an hour before he'd taken off for Tampa.

In addition to hacking the El Perro Perdido website, Pepe had also asked Jorge to hack into the background of Jeremy Harlan.

It was a dangerous request for Detective Torentez. Police officers did not do background checks on each other, especially partners.

The rap sheet, printed and folded in half, glared up at him in stark, white fact.

From the moment he'd met Jeremy, leaning against the chrome countertop at his favorite bar, he's known there was something different, and dangerous about him. *But was it evil?*

Only weeks ago Jeremy had put bullets through four drug dealers without blinking an eye, laughing with the rest of them over flutes of champagne later that same night. *Was that evil?*

The man was his best friend, the would-be god-father of his child. He desperately wanted to believe he had nothing to do with the grisly murders, but every time he tried to give him the benefit of doubt, the man just went and acted weirder. Now, looking at the information Jorge had discovered in his records, it was getting very real.

Pepe scanned over each arrest, the number of incidents alarming. Some were typical teenage pranks, others more sinister. The one that stood out related to a veterinary clinic. Pepe read the police report and was horrified by the words on the page. The clinic had been owned by a John Harlan, who Pepe assumed was Jeremy's father. Jeremy had never opened up about his family, but unless he'd dropped out of a UFO, he had to have one. It also explained why the case had been buried, without any charges filed. But what kind of kid would harm innocent, animals... animals that were already sick or dying? *A serial killer?*

The thought sent a shiver down his spine, which he quickly brushed to one side. As sickening as that discovery had been, it was nothing to compared to the small line of information Pepe's eyes now fell upon.

The planes tires hit the runway, jostling Pepe and the papers balanced atop his open notebook. At the same instant everything went white, and Pepe heard a slight buzzing in his ears.

It appeared that Jorge had been able to hack into rescuegy's Web browser history, and an online form he'd filled out when searching for flights to Cuba. Jorge explained that while the user had never actually sent the request, Jorge was able to hack the characters he had typed inside the information boxes. In the credit card section, a name had appeared.

*J. Harlan.*

"There is a Chief Roland out here, sir."

The voice came abruptly from the pilot, standing in the door of the plane.

Pepe looked up at him, with tears in his eyes.

"Are you alright, sir?"

He blinked down at the page in his hand, his fingers trembling. *No, no, no!*

*Yes.* And in some way, he'd known, hadn't he? Otherwise why did he find himself in Tampa, spending valuable investigative resources uncovering his partner's past, when there was a killer on the loose.

Pepe felt he was going to be sick, and the walls of the plane seemed to suddenly start shrinking.

"Sir, do you need a moment?"

He found it in himself to nod, once, and the officer went away.

When Pepe emerged from the plane, he'd at least managed to wipe his face, but could only imagine what he might look like to the giant figure waiting beside a gleaming pick up. Walking towards him with an air of wariness, he put one big fist forward to shake Pepe's hand. On his finger glistened a huge signet with fine cut stones. It looked like a Super Bowl ring.

Roland invited Pepe to take a seat inside his car, wasting little time before he launched into his offensive.

"Look, son, don't come down here to my town acting like you are slick as pig shit. I may be retired, but I can smell Brutus behind me."

The retired chief was massive, and mad. They didn't like detectives coming around and digging up old cases; it led to trouble that they'd thought they'd left behind. When Roland demanded to know the reason for Pepe's visit, he'd made some vague statement about an old, unimportant case and a favor for a friend. Now that he was facing the man, confined inside a truck cabin, Pepe dreaded telling Roland what he knew he must. But if Pepe was going to take down his best friend as a cold blooded murderer, he needed to know what he was dealing with. Roland seemed like the only person who might be able to give him some straight answers.

Pepe shifted his tie and tried to gather up the nerve to speak, but he never got the chance. Roland sat back and said in his husky voice, "You're here about Jeremy Harlan, aren't you son?"

# CHAPTER FIFTY-FIVE

Monica felt strange arriving back home.

As she locked her car and walked inside, she said the word aloud. "Home." It sounded sad, more a wish than a reality. Without Jeremy, her treasured little beach condo was just walls and a roof.

Monica was feeling a lot of things, beside this swelling sense of pain. Exhaustion, coupled with a strange kind of anxiety that wouldn't let her rest. And then, beyond the sadness, worry and fatigue, something even more debilitating.

Fear.

It clung to her like an invisible cloak, stayed close around her as she opened the kitchen door. She could not explain it.

Then there was Grady. He always been able to take her mind off things, but as she shut the door she found herself walking straight past him, barely aware of the heavy tail thumping against her calves.

Monica placed her keys on the rack by the washroom door and slung her purse over a chair as she reached the dining room table. She went to switch on the lights, then she sensed it.

Something was behind her.

Monica jerked around, expecting to see a tall, dark figure looming towards her, but there was only Grady, his ecstatic tail thumping reduced to a slow, dejected twitch.

Hand on heart, she flicked the light switch on and took a deep breath as the shadows disappeared. But still, she could feel it. Like nothing she had experienced before, the inexplicable presence stayed with her in the room.

Monica did not believe in ghosts, but this was enough to make her change her mind. Feeling overwhelmed, she opened the bottom oven and reached for the pistol, relieved to find it still there.

"Thank God," she whispered.

She was too scared to feel as silly as she probably looked, lurching around the empty house with gun drawn, but *something* was in there with her. She looked over and saw Grady still standing by the dining room table, aware that she had totally forgotten to let him out. He simply sat, watching her, as if unsure of what was going on and waiting for instruction.

Monica looked into his sad brown eyes. "Come here, Grady. Come here, boy."

Grady was very happy to oblige his mother. He ran around the island stove, turning the corner to get to Monica, and as he did he slid sideways, bumping the chair in front of the computer. The chair tipped, causing the back to topple against the keyboard.

Monica slowly stood, staring at the top left corner of the screen. The window was open, showing the mail account she'd created for 'Lulusmom', Carrie Powell.

The small envelope icon sat there, static and deadly. It instantly explained the evil feeling in her house. Without opening the email she knew this was him…The Lost Dog Killer. Without thinking she pointed the gun at the monitor, and then realized what she was doing. But she could not help it. Her finger twitched at the trigger, longing to fire through the screen, as if that might end the nightmare once and for all.

Monica laid the pistol down, reluctantly, and slid into her computer chair, directing her cursor to the Inbox tab.

She clicked.

The message was from the El Perro Perdido Web site, and even though she'd known it would be, her heart skipped a beat.

> *Lulu's Mom,*
>
> *I believe I've found your dog! Such a cute little thing, too. I can tell she misses you.*

*Don't worry, I am taking great care of her, and await your e-mail. And hey, let's have a celebratory drink after meeting up? A dog this cute must have a pretty gorgeous Momma too!*

*Daniel*

*PS: I know a great 'dog friendly' bar near my house, so dress to party!*

Monica felt frightened, but beneath her fear was a large dose of disgust. The hypocrisy of "Daniel's" kind reassurance, the sleaziness in suggesting she wear something "celebratory"...it was beyond evil.

She picked up her cell phone and sent a text to Pepe.

*He wrote me, it's him. Call me.*

A moment later Pepe's name was flashing across her screen.

# CHAPTER FIFTY-SIX

"Read it to me, Mamita. Read me the email."

Once she'd finished Pepe informed her he was returning from the airport and would soon be at her house. Thankfully, Monica didn't question where he'd been.

When Pepe arrived at her house he immediately noticed the pistol lying next to her computer. He'd already taken a quick glance in the garage and noted that Jeremy's car wasn't inside, but he still had to ask.

"Is Jeremy home?"

Monica tore her eyes away from the monitor to look at him, before quickly glancing away.

"No."

Pepe scanned the email over her shoulder. From the moment she'd read it to him on the phone, he'd known it wasn't Jeremy. It simply didn't resemble the other messages victims had received, and the username was different, leading him to think it was either a legitimate message, or simply a lonely guy trying to pick up a heartbroken woman. Of course, Monica had no way of knowing this, as Pepe hadn't shared Jorge's findings with her.

But now that he knew the unthinkable truth, how could he tell her? Monica loved Jeremy in the same way Shelly loved him. Devoted, blind to his many faults and weaknesses. If he told her what he'd found, there was every chance she'd refuse to believe it, and potentially blow the whole case wide open by running to him at the first chance.

She wanted to write back to the "killer" right away, and began typing a response. Pepe stopped her.

"Hang on there, Monica. We need to be strategic with this."

Fingers hovering over the keyboard, she frowned in impatience. "I know what to do. Everything I've done so far has worked out. You want to get this guy, don't you?"

Pepe stalled for as long as possible, talking about procedures and permissions, before finally realizing that setting up a sting for the wrong guy may in fact be a good practice run for Monica. It would also provide the distraction required to keep her from discovering the truth.

Then a new idea flashed into his mind. What if, instead of keeping everything under wraps, Pepe instead *told* Jeremy about Monica's ad? Conclusive evidence implicated Jeremy in the murders. But Pepe still couldn't quite believe it, and knew he wouldn't be sure until he'd seen some sign of guilt from the man himself. This would finally decide it. Killer or not, Pepe knew that Jeremy loved Monica. If Jeremy heard the news of his wife's involvement without blinking, it meant he knew she was in no real danger, proving he was The Lost Dog Killer. If he was innocent, Pepe had no doubt Jeremy would go off the rails, accusing him of making his wife a target. It was perfect.

"I've changed my mind," Pepe said to a confused Monica. "Go ahead and answer back, like we talked about before. But let's beat him to the punch and suggest a park before he does, so we can have more control of the set up."

"Great idea."

Pepe helped Monica fill out the information until they were both satisfied, and then Monica sent it off into the cyber wilderness.

She sat back in her chair, only to jump as Grady nudged her thigh with his nose. "Oh Grady, come on boy. I am sooo sorry!"

She jumped up, running around the island to open the sliding glass door to the patio, and allowing Grady to go do his thing.

Pepe watched her staring outside, waiting for the dog, and felt a terrible pang at the sight. Was this what awaited her in the future? He felt terribly afraid for her, not because of anything Jeremy might do, but for the life that would meet her when, or *if* he corrected, Jeremy was convicted. The media attention would be brutal, the court trial long and painful, and then what? A life with Grady?

Would they visit Jeremy in jail, and still think of him as their friend, albeit a psychotic one? He had to accept that Jeremy was sick; he was sure of that after his trip to Tampa. Talking to Chief Roland had left him feeling sorry for the boy Jeremy had been, and the man, and killer, he had become.

Pepe took a look at the computer monitor while Monica was outside with Grady.

No mail.

Monica slid the door shut behind Grady and walked back to him. Pepe glanced at the pistol, still lying beside her keyboard, then looked up with his brows raised.

"I get scared sometimes, that's all."

Pepe couldn't mask his surprise. Had Jeremy threatened her, after all?

"Did he do something to scare you?"

In an instant her eyes narrowed, and she slowly shook her head.

"Who, Jeremy?"

Pepe shrugged.

"Why would you think Jeremy would scare me?"

As soon as she said the words Pepe turned away, but not before he caught a look of surprise flash across Monica's features.

"Jeremy is a good man, Pepe."

He nodded, fighting the sudden impulse to break down and spill his guts about all that he'd discovered. But he couldn't.

"He's just going through something hard right now, that's all. He'll return to us soon."

"Of cour—" Pepe chocked the words out, but was suddenly interrupted by the chime of her computer, notifying them that she had new email.

The sting had begun.

# CHAPTER FIFTY-SEVEN

The clock on the microwave read 8:36P.M. Monica knew it was time for her to get in her car and head for Cutler Ridge Park. She dressed herself in figure-hugging yoga pants, jogging bra and a tight tank top.

Years ago, when they'd first started dating, Jeremy had told her he wanted her to always wear tight-fitting clothes when jogging. It was a strange request from a man who was prone to jealousy, and she'd looked at him with her brow raised, stating that as a Latina her clothes sat pretty firm, anyway. Did he really want them tighter? Jeremy had run his hands up her sides, setting her skin on fire and whispering, "You know I love you...I have never liked the way other men look at you."

"So why the clothes then?"

"Because if some guy every tries to grab you, and I'm not there to rip his arm off, it will give him less to grip on to."

He'd murmured the words against her ear, dark and dangerous, and she'd almost melted on the spot. But for all her raging hormones, she'd never forgotten the advice and tonight it seemed she'd be putting it to use.

Pepe had provided her with an envelope of money, and she placed it in her backpack along with Grady's leash. Her fingers were shaking as she zipped the bag shut, and she hoped that if they made a successful arrest tonight, the constant paranoia that had plagued her of late might finally come to an end.

She was sick of lying in bed certain she was being watched, and yet unable to close the bedroom door. With it open, she could see her computer monitor from her pillow, and that was where the problem lay. She needed to see any message that came in, but it always felt as if the computer monitor could see her from its nook in the kitchen, too.

When she'd finished packing she knelt down to pray, only to find a wet nose intrude upon her solemn words. She patted Grady. "I'll be back, boy, I'll be back."

The words were more for her than for him, a prayer in their own right.

She stood up and walked out to her car, surprised by the voice that appeared in her ear. "Grady is a lucky boy."

Jumping, she realized Pepe was talking to her from down the car parked down the street. She had forgotten the earpiece tucked inside her ear, and the microphone secured between her cleavage.

"Oh gosh, you startled me, Pepe!"

"Well I'm glad you can hear me, and I can hear you just fine. You okay?"

"Yeah, I'm good."

"Well, we all prayed with you a moment ago, just so you know. Did you forget you were mic'd?"

"Yeah," she said, feeling a lot less like a detective, and a lot more like a young, frightened woman.

"Everything will be fine, you have nothing to fear."

Monica wondered how Pepe could sound so confident when she was walking straight into the path of a man who'd killed four women.

She backed up the rental car Pepe's men had dropped off, that had been waiting for her in Jeremy's spot inside the garage. After Pepe told her of Jeremy's reaction to the plan she'd known he wouldn't be coming home, but she wondered if he planned on joining them in the sting. Pepe had said he wouldn't be, but her heart held out hope.

She turned the Buick LaSabre into drive and headed east toward the park.

"Just drive normal, Mamita."

"You won't pull me over for speeding, will you?" She gave a light laugh, and was immediately aware of how nervous it sounded. Pulling a stick of gum from her bag on the passenger seat, she stuck it in her mouth, chewing furiously and releasing a series of small, snappy bubbles.

"*Epa, epa*, that is loud, Mamita!"

"Sorry!"

"All good, we got you covered. We've done this plenty of times."

She was now turning west on Cutler Ridge Drive, about two miles from the park. The dashboard clock read 8:42P.M., the meeting scheduled for a quarter to.

As she headed down Cutler Ridge, Monica glanced in her rear vision mirror at the car that was tailing her.

"Do you guys want to back off a bit? I mean, I know I am not a pro at this, but if I can tell you are following me, then this guy might notice as well."

"Don't worry about us, Monica, just focus on what you need to do."

She put on her blinker and turned left into the park. The parking lot was large and divided into two sections that were split by a long island of trees. She pulled into the second entrance to the soccer fields, where the meeting was to take place. The car tailing her had kept going a bit, illuminated a large area with its brake lights. Further away, a second car loitered as well. They may as well form a procession!

"Do you guys have to be so obvious, Pepe?"

"You are doing fine, Mamita."

"Yeah, but your guys are going to blow this, I swear!"

"Just get out and walk to the grove of trees, as discussed."

Monica exited the car, leaving her bag and carrying only the newly purchased leash, as well as her envelope of cash. Eyes wide and mouth open, she began walking toward the soccer fields, passing between the swimming pool locker rooms on her right and the smaller pavilion on her left.

She knew she was acting scared, but she could not help it.

As she made her way through the two buildings she came to a brief opening before the grove of trees. Beyond lay the soccer field. In the distance near the trees stood a figure, a long, red dog leash hanging from his hand. At the end of it was a dog, just like the one she had posted in her listing. *Odd.* She hadn't expected that.

With all the mental strength she could muster, she commanded her body to continue moving toward the man and the small, brown companion. Each step was hell, but she kept telling herself that the men following behind were so close they wouldn't let anything happen.

185

But something was wrong.
Something was very wrong.

# CHAPTER FIFTY-EIGHT

The man waved at her enthusiastically, his eyes raking up her figure.

"Hi!" he called. "Wow, Mommy is as gorgeous as her baby…"

Monica grimaced, but continued to move forward. The guy was medium height, with a cheesy grin and eighties workout clothes. He seemed awful, but relatively harmless. Was it all an act?

When she was only about ten feet away, she caught a flash of movement in her peripheral vision, and suddenly realized that the sicko might not be working alone. Her fears seemed to be confirmed when she turned and saw three guys marching toward her from across the street.

"Oh, I see you brought some company," the dog guy said. "That's no fun. I was hoping we might party a bit. I got some pills, and some powder…"

She looked back at the guy and realized they must be cops. *Dammit*. Why was Pepe blowing her cover now, before the guy'd had a chance to make his move?

"What are you doing?" she hissed into the microphone, turning her body away from Dog Guy and towards the men.

"What are you talking about?"

"The three cops marching toward me from the pool building!"

"What the hell is going on?" Dog Guy marched up to her and handed her the leash. "Here, take your dog, I don't want it. The reward however…"

Confused, she took the leash and stood there as they looked towards the men approaching. Suddenly, Dog Guy decided he didn't want the reward after all, and scurried off into the trees.

"What cops?" Pepe's words brought her back into reality.

The men were much closer now, only thirty or so meters away. At this distance she could tell they weren't cops. If anything, they looked like gang members.

Pepe's frantic order for his officers to get on the scene where the last thing Monica heard before the smallest of the men had walked right up to her and knocked her off her feet.

"Hey—" she started, before realizing that he and his friend had guns pointed in her face; the other thug pulling out a roll of duct tape. He ripped a strip free and stepped towards her, but before her could put it across her mouth the taller man standing at her side collapsed. Belatedly, Monica noted the *pop, pop, pop* of gun shots coming from underneath the trees. Another series of shots and the man holding the tape suddenly sunk to his knees beside his friend.

The smallest one, still holding his pistol, stepped back from Monica as if she were possessed by some kind of demon.

"Damario? Phoenix!"

He looked up from his friend, his head whipping around to see where the shots had come from. Then he started running, right into the arms of the undercover unit. Six cops held their badges out, with pistols pointed. They yelled various words in different languages, all with the same meaning: *Stop!*

He ran on, as if deaf to their words, gun thrust out before him and blue fire sparking with each round he fired. A moment later he was face down in the grass, dead.

Monica was on her knees, tears rolling down her cheeks as the shock began to turn to utter confusion.

"What ... what happened?"

She took the earpiece out and threw it at Pepe, overcome with inexplicable anger. "You idiot! What did you do?" Pepe tried to grab her, but she jerked away from him.

"Monica, listen to me. I don't know what happened."

They looked at the bodies around them, as if trying to find some sign of recognition, but there was none. Then the blood, and gore, became too much. She jumped to her feet like someone zapped her, quickly stepping away from them.

"Who are they Pepe? Three killers, rather than one? It doesn't make sense..."

"I know, but we will find out, Monica." He tried to steady her with his hands, but again she jerked away. "We'll have answers soon, I promise."

A series of squad cars pulled up around the field and began swarming the area. Some appeared to be searching, others were standing around the bodies, marking off the area as a crime scene. A young female officer appeared from nowhere, putting a blanket around Monica's shoulders and gently pulling the leash from her hand. Monica had entirely forgotten about the small dog at her side, and watched as it trotted off towards a squad car.

She was about to ask what they planned on doing with it, the question a welcome distraction from the darker thoughts currently swirling around her mind, when a young detective walked up to Pepe with a phone in his hand.

"It's Chief Dorsey. He wants to know who fired the first shots."

Pepe shook his head. "I don't know," he said. "No one in our team."

He took the phone and stared at it, as if it were a live grenade. Monica placed her hand gently on his arm and said in an undertone, "I know who shot them. I saw him."

Pepe looked at her in confusion, then his face cleared and darkened, all at once. He'd guessed before she said the words.

"It was Jeremy."

# CHAPTER FIFTY-NINE

Pepe had never strung so many expletives together as he did standing over the bodies of the dead men. He had no idea who they were, only that the night had raised a lot more questions than it had answered.

"Monica, are you sure it was Jeremy?" There was no point asking. Even if she hadn't seen him with her own eyes, there was only one cop in their precinct whose aim was good enough to down three men from that distance.

"Yes, I saw him."

Pepe turned to the cops standing around them. "Did anyone else see him?"

No one responded.

"Well, then where the hell is he?"

As if God where answering himself, the radio on Pepe's belt burst into life.

*"Four-Fifteen to Master Sergeant, Four-Fifteen to Master Sergeant."*

Pepe unclipped the unit and raised it to his lips. "Go ahead David, what have you got?"

"Sir, I have a white male in custody. Possibly the perp, sir."

He almost asked if it was Jeremy Harlan, but stopped himself. "What's your twenty, David?"

*"I've sighted you, sir. Coming to you now."*

Officer David approached them with a man whose arms where cuffed behind his back. As they got closer, Monica said, "That's the guy. He was here waiting by the trees when I came over, before these other men tried to grab me."

Pepe grabbed a flashlight and shone it in the suspect's face. "You know these two men?"

The man was scared and shaking, and probably high on some type of narcotic.

"*No*, man! No, I swear. I just wanted to party, that's all. I swear!"

Pepe had dealt with enough bad guys to recognize a young, harmless punk when he saw one. He was a creep, but he wasn't a murderer, or even a dealer.

He turned to the officer. "Where is Jeremy?"

"As in Detective Harlan?"

Pepe groaned in frustration.

"No, Jeremy Cricket, you idiot!"

Officer David blushed. "Uh, I think you mean Jiminy Cricket, sir."

"You know what I mean!"

David smirked at his angry superior. "I didn't see Detective Harlan, sir," he said, lowering his chin and cutting his eyes back up at Pepe. "But I guess if he were here that would explain a lot."

"Like what?"

The officer laughed. "Why I found this man handcuffed to a lamppost out there, with the keys hanging 'round his neck."

Pepe spent the next two hours on the scene, before going back to the precinct to meet with Chief Dorsey. He kept Monica with him the entire time, and together they spent almost the entire night trying to make sense of the recent events, without luck.

The Medical Examiner took fingerprints of the three dead men, as well as the still-living, and very confused, man they'd found handcuffed to the lamppost. Pepe and Dorsey guessed the dead perps were hit men, though they didn't think their intent had been to kill, nor did they match the style of assaults committed by The Lost Dog Killer in any way. They'd each had a .9mm, equipped with a silencer. One of the men carried duct tape, cable ties, a box cutter and a sock; it was a clearly a kidnapping gone bad.

The intent might have been apparent, but when it came to motive, Dorsey and Pepe were lost. Why would anyone want to kidnap Monica?

As the sun began to rise on a new day, Monica sat sipping tea and Pepe and the chief read through a stack of files. A desk officer walked up and handed Pepe a slip of paper. He tried to show no expression and managed it well, though Monica seemed too tired to really notice what he was doing anyway. Jeremy had disappeared, and her mind was elsewhere.

Pepe needed to talk to Dorsey about the information on the sheet of paper, and he knew Monica was in no shape to hear it. He turned and touched her gently on the arm. "Mamita, it's almost morning. Why don't you go home, huh? I'll park two officers outside."

"Jeremy..."

She didn't finish the thought, and they both knew the truth. He wouldn't be at their home, and if he was, no one knew what kind of confrontation awaited her. What she didn't know, and what Pepe had just been informed of, was that Monica had become a target to a whole new threat.

Monica accepted his offer of protection, letting the blanket wrapped around her shoulders fall back onto the chair. Once on her feet she stumbled slightly, and one of the admin ladies rushed forward to help her. A glance from Pepe to the woman confirmed that she was not to drive herself home.

She was well out of sight when Dorsey said, "Okay, what's on that sheet?"

Pepe didn't want to read it again, so he chose to paraphrase. "Monica's parents, well, her foster parents, were found murdered out in California yesterday."

Dorsey was emotionless. "Was it a robbery?"

"I don't think so. The prints from that crime scene match our prints here."

"What?" Dorsey's eyes were wide. "Pepe what the hell is going on here?"

"Chief, at this point aliens could drop from the sky and I wouldn't blink an—"

"We've got names!" a desk officer shouted, leaving Pepe with his hands flung open in exasperation.

Pepe and Dorsey ran to the officer's desk to view his screen. They had never heard of Damario, Phoenix, or Ciro. But the three men now lying in the morgue were very familiar to the DEA and FBI.

Pepe pushed himself away from the screen and began walking in small circles between the desks.

"This is more complicated than trying to balance my wife's checkbook! What could these three have to do with the Lost Dog Killer?"

A part of him couldn't help wondering if Jeremy was somehow involved, as if he'd somehow guessed they were on his trail, and thrown in a bucket full of red herrings to throw them off. *But to murder her parents?*

"Try calling Jeremy again, Pepe. Tell him we have positive IDs on the men he shot. See if he calls us back."

# CHAPTER SIXTY

Monica stepped out of the shower, partly revived after forty-five minutes of scalding water running over her body. Eventually it had run cold, and reluctantly she'd stepped out. She got herself dried off and slid into her favorite cotton nightgown, unable to remember the last time she'd felt so tired, if ever.

A soft call to Grady brought him leaping onto the bed, clearly happy to break the rules while the master was away. Her fingers found the switch for the lamp, and as she switched the light off she was suddenly aware of it...that same eerie feeling that she was being watched. Monica shrugged it off, telling herself her mind was playing tricks, a result of her exhaustion.

She was just reaching to up to pull the blanket up over her legs when her eyes drifted over and locked upon the computer monitor. The small rectangle of light caught her gaze and wouldn't release it.

Her eyes scanned everything around her, like radar. She seemed to be on high alert, as if detecting something beyond the five senses. Monica was learning to trust her instincts.

She put her feet back onto the floor, neglecting to turn the lamp back on, and walked out of the bedroom into the den.

"Jeremy, is that you?"

There was no answer.

Monica moved to the kitchen window and glanced at the police vehicle that was parked outside. It was dark, and she couldn't see much, but her imagination ran wild. Were the officers sitting out there with their throats slashed? She wanted to call to them, but convinced herself she was being stupid.

"Come here, Grady."

She heard the tags on his collar jingle and his big body thump to the ground. Within seconds, he was right by her side.

Walking past the dining room table, Monica found herself drawn once more to the monitor. Tentatively, her finger pushed the mouse, and with a little jolt the screen flashed up to reveal the desktop photo of herself and Jeremy sitting on the beach in front of their house.

She only looked at their bright, happy faces for a moment before noticing she had new mail. Or, to be accurate, Carrie Powell had new mail.

It was a response to her posting from a new person who had apparently thought they'd found her dog. Monica tapped her chin, trying to make sense of the name.

Rescuegy.

Never before had Monica experienced such a transformation. It almost felt like a miracle. In seconds, her mind and body shifted from fear and exhaustion, to anger. Pure, unadulterated rage, hot and explosive as a rumbling volcano.

This person had chosen to stalk his victims inside their own homes. And now he was stalking her at this very moment. This was how he watched them, chose them, a predator picking off the weaker ones from the edge of the pack.

He preyed upon the hurt of loss, the ache of loneliness. This was not about sex, or power. He was simply putting them down, because he could.

Monica let the anger build inside her, let it simmer and boil until her finger nails began to cut into the soft flesh of her palms. This was the one, this was the Lost Dog Killer.

Her heartbeat told her so.

And she was ready for him. She began typing her e-mail response, letting the happiness and gratitude of a woman finding her pet flow into her words. Praising him for finding her baby, she told him she would meet him anytime, anywhere, and the sooner the better. Monica sent the e-mail with a click of the mouse, then, seeing it was very early in the morning, went to switch the computer off and finally sink into her bed.

*Bing.*

Someone may as well have traced an ice cube down the curve of her spine.

The reply read:

*Hi Carrie,*

> *Vizcaya Museum and Gardens is on South Miami Ave. It is a beautiful spot with lots of trees. If you have never been you will find it very peaceful. It's an historical landmark and museum and most importantly, a safe place to meet. I will be there tomorrow night at nine o'clock. Don't worry about your little Lulu; she is in the best of care here. I run a rescue for dogs and a refugee for all types of animals in need. Let me know if that time works, and I will see you then. My name is Michael.*

Monica paused a moment, and imagine what she would write if the situation were 'real'. Finally, she settled with:

> *Thank God for people like you, people who care. Michael, you are a wonderful human being! I will be there and right on time. Thank you, thank you, thank you!*

It was a little over the top, but then that probably only made her more attractive to him. Surprising herself, instead of hovering around she was content to switch the computer off and march back into her bedroom, Grady at her heels. Where was the sick feeling, the crippling fear? It was gone, replaced by something else that was much tougher, and a lot less forgiving. She was going to see this to the end; would stare at the killer when he sat behind bars, and laugh in his face.

# CHAPTER SIXTY-ONE

Dorsey and Pepe were still at the precinct when the two uniforms responsible for watching Monica reported in after their shift.

"Everything was quiet, no sign of anything unusual. She seems sweet, Mrs. Harlan, if a bit sad. She brought us coffee this morning then went out around lunchtime. Sanchez and Brior are on duty now, they tailed her."

The second officer decided to chime in. "Yeah, Harlan's wife is beautiful. Seems so soft for a guy like Jeremy."

Pepe's heavy brows drew together. "Speaking of Detective Harlan, did he ever show up?"

The officers answered in unison: "No sir."

"Good job, men, take off."

Pepe flipped his cell phone open, scrolling down to Monica's number. He had to break the news to her about her parents, before the media, or a concerned loved one or friend beat him to it. He could only guess how she might take it, given everything else going on, but the best he could do was have her come into the precinct with Shelly. Together, they would support her. The dial tone ended with her voicemail message.

"Hey, Mamita. I am still here at the office. Just checking in to see how you are after last night. I told Shelly to take you out for lunch, so I hope that's where you are. Can you call me when you get a chance? Something's come up." He scrolled down to Shelly's number and dialed, but there was no answer there either. They'd be drinking coffee at Arlo's, most likely.

Pepe rubbed his eyes, scratchy from thirty-six hours without sleep. He had an AWOL partner and two murders in California, connected to his partner's wife. If that weren't enough, there was every chance that missing partner, and his best friend, was in fact a psychopathic serial killer.

Or was he?

None of it made any sense. Jeremy clearly hadn't turned up at the park last night to kill his wife; he'd saved her. But then why was he running? Was he chasing someone, or being chased? Could he have somehow become mixed up in the drug cartels, was there a narcotics link they'd missed?

There were times when Pepe questioned bringing a child into such a world.

He needed answers, and the only way he knew to get them was to ask. Pepe just wasn't sure how. He tried calling Jeremy again, and again got his voicemail, which was now full due to all of the messages Pepe had left him. With a final sigh of resignation he ordered dispatch to put out an APB out on Detective Jeremy Harlan, wanted for questioning concerning the Lost Dog Killer. Then he scheduled a press conference for the following morning. This would give him enough time to talk to Monica before she heard all the latest developments on the news. They wouldn't tell the media everything, but too much had gone down to remain silent any longer.

As a final thought, he ordered an undercover unit to trail Monica, along with the two cops who were overtly protecting her. Jeremy had been following his wife last night, and there was a chance he still was. If the undercover guys hung back far enough, they just might catch him slinking around the edges of the scene, where he liked it best.

Monica had managed to hide two things from Shelly. The hardest was the fact that she knew Shelly was pregnant, but equally distracting was that she was going to meet a serial killer later that evening. It's no surprise that she hadn't acted like her usual self, and when her best friend dropped her home, only to have her lurch out of the car without so much as a goodbye flung over her shoulder, Shelly could do little more than sigh, and send a text to her husband telling him he better be taking good care of her girl.

It was 7:45 p.m. when Monica hurried inside and walked to the laundry, pulling her clothes out of the dryer from the night before. She put them on, then turned her attention to the backpack. It held the exact same contents as it had twenty-four hours earlier. She unzipped the pack, looking over the mace, the leash and finally the wireless transmitter. Removing it from the pack, she placed it on the kitchen countertop. She wouldn't be using it, this time.

Monica started to zip her bag shut but paused, glancing over at the computer monitor. Still turned towards the wall, so that it couldn't 'watch her', she suffered a faint shiver down her spine and walked to the over to retrieve the pistol, before placing it inside her bag as well. This time, there would be no army of policeman, with crackling radios and lurking shadows. Monica would have to be her own back up, and while that thought might have terrified her only yesterday, on this day, she was a different woman. The Lost Dog Killer had preyed on women looking for help and comfort, and lured them to their doom. But this time he had baited one who knew what she was up against, and was angry enough to burn down all of Miami. She didn't return Pepe's calls, or several others that had appeared on her phone from various friends and family. Nor did she tell Jeremy of her plan. She wasn't going to allow anyone to screw this up for her.

With a glance through the front window at the cops sitting outside, she turned the TV on loud and slunk out the back door with her bag slung over her shoulder. From there, it was only a short jog down the beach to the bus stop, where she could catch a direct line into town. Perhaps it was madness to go without any kind of backup, but Monica knew she couldn't live another moment with the pervasive sense of evil looming over her. Or the knowledge that every delay, and failed attempt, could mean another woman killed. This was her chance, and if the monster sensed they were onto him, he might slip out of their grasp forever.

# CHAPTER SIXTY-TWO

Monica was very familiar with the Vizcaya Museum, in fact it was one of her favorite places to take Grady for a walk. The south garden was a peaceful place to sit and admire the gorgeous architecture of the Vizcaya home, and she was relieved "Michael" had requested it as their meeting place.

The area he'd proposed was not far from the maze garden, which Grady loved to romp around. Except now, instead of being filled with barking dogs, puffing joggers and squealing children, it was dark and quiet.

Even at night it was beautiful though, the air heavy with the scent of flowering shrubs wet grass. And the quiet allowed her to listen, and detect movement around her, even if it was hard to see beyond the occasional pool of lamplight.

The gardens had been built with a structure specifically for plants to grow on, the walls made of stone. It was a blueprint for the secret garden she fantasized about having someday, created by James Deering, who'd wanted a living temple to honor his orchids. Deering had grown them in a shade house located in the village across the street, back in the early 1900s. Monica could admire a man like that. A man who celebrated his life, rather than battled through it.

But there was no time to think about that now, as she stood outside the museum. She gripped the backpack with one hand, carrying it down by her knees as she began to walk around the side of the museum. Pausing to raise the pack up against her belly, she unzipped it a little to provide easy access to the gun, if she needed it.

Somehow she knew that it was not a question of *if*, but *when*, and yet she felt eerily calm.

Making her way around to the back of the museum, she walked past the maze garden. She had passed between the hedges so many times with Grady and was comforted by the thought that if she needed to flee, a chase through the maze would probably work to her advantage; she knew it like the back of her hand.

It wasn't so dark that she couldn't see, and there were several soft floodlights scattered around the secret garden, but they were largely covered by vegetation and the moon was waning. The garden was famous for the beautiful archway leading to its stairs, which formed the dark setting of their meeting place. Monica stood on the sidewalk waiting, realizing that she had not seen any cars in the parking lot when she'd walked in. She raised her arm to look at her watch, and that was when she felt it. The dark, almost intoxicating sense of being watched by someone, something, evil.

Slowly, carefully she began to turn around, slipping her hand into the gun in her bag. He was nearby, she knew it, but suddenly she was distracted by a sting at her neck. Monica assumed it was an insect, but fought the instinct to slap it away and instead kept her hand on the gun. The only problem was her hand no longer wanted to cooperate, and she watched with a vague sense of horror as the bag, with her gun, dropped uselessly to the concrete pavers. A moment later, her body followed.

Monica didn't feel the impact, but she watched it, noting the odd jarring effect of her head bouncing a few times before settling. Then, her mind started to drift off in search of her body. She could smell flowers, thousands of them, and blinked a few times, trying to see the beautiful colors that awaited...somewhere nearby.

Instead all she could see were a pair of black shoes and behind them, a figure running across the grass. She could recognize that long, powerful stride anywhere and tried to call out to him, but her lips wouldn't move. Oddly, she couldn't seem to breathe either.

She saw the man sprinting, faster and faster. She was trying to call his name, *Daddy, Daddy!*

The words wouldn't come out.

As the figure finally reached her the shoes turned, and she watched as the two men-- one larger than the other--fell to their knees, and then their backs, rolling and struggling as if wrestling for life itself.

*How silly*, Monica thought.

In the distance, a third figure was sprinting towards them, but he would come too late. The bigger man had gained the upper hand, a giant compared to the form underneath him. One brutal blow was delivered after another, the monster effortlessly taking control. Monica watched with a vague sense of dismay as the silver flash of a knife appeared to hover, the victor raising it above him as if to strike.

*No!* Monica longed to say. But it was no use. The big man was simply too strong.

# CHAPTER SIXTY-THREE

Pepe entered the park with his gun drawn, and a very strong feeling that someone was going to die. He just hoped it wasn't himself.

It all seemed so surreal, that he could find himself in a park stalking his best friend, who was at this moment probably trying to murder an innocent woman. He breathed deep in an effort to still the jitters. When he'd gone to the chief asking for access to the mobile tracking software, he'd hoped to locate Jeremy somewhere quiet. For all he'd done, the man was still like a brother to him, and the least he could do was spare Monica the further shock of an arrest with twenty cops and a SWAT team in tow. Hopping in the car, he'd turned on the small tablet and waited for the beacon to appear on its screen. When it started flashing in Viscaya Park, Pepe's blood ran cold. Jeremy was out hunting.

He'd called in back up but they were still minutes away. Passing the hedge maze, he glared at the small, blue screen in his hand, wary of the fact it was illuminating him in what was otherwise a very dark night. If there was one thing he knew about Jeremy, it was that the man could out-shoot, out-run and out-fight him, any day of the week. It didn't seem fair to crunch through the dark as a big, glowing target.

Ahead, towards the entry arch, an object caught his eye. With a low hiss of surprise he saw a woman sprawled on her side, right on the edge of a street lamp's dim light. Her thick, silky hair was fanned across the grass. It was Monica.

"No!" he cried, leaping forward. As he fell to his knees beside her lifeless body he gave a loud cry of despair. Somehow he'd accepted the fact his best friend was a serial killer, but that he'd hurt Monica? That was unthinkable.

Before he could start CPR a grunting sound made him look up and into the darkness. A small, Hispanic man with salt and pepper hair was crawling towards them.

"Pepita! My child!"

Pepe instinctively pushed him away, but the man wouldn't stand for it.

"Is she alive?" He put his bloody fingers on her throat. "Please don't leave us baby!" A large gash bled from his head, and looked like a knife wound. Pepe frantically glanced around, pointing his gun into the deep black of the night. That was when he saw him. About five meters away and lost in the shadows of a large hedge, was Jeremy. He wasn't alone.

Pepe's partner was on his back, a large man bent over him with a hunting knife pressed at his throat. Jeremy had both hands locked on the man's wrists, but it was clear it was a losing battle.

"Police!" He strode towards them. "Drop the knife and raise your hands."

Jeremy's attacker glanced at Pepe, and he was shocked to see an older version of his friend looking back at him. The same cold blue eyes and arrogant chin, but softened slightly by time. It was uncanny.

"Shoot him," Jeremy hissed, his arms trembling with exertion. Pepe's gun swayed between them. Had the older gents had come across Jeremy assaulting his wife and intervened? Or were they implicated too, somehow? A thousand conflicting possibilities arose and Pepe clenched the gun in confusion, unsure where to point it.

"Pepe!" Jeremy started groaning as the large man atop him hunched his shoulders forward and put his full weight upon the blade.

Pepe lifted his handgun to the sky, but before he could fire off a warning round Jeremy brought up his knee, hard into his attacker's back. The man fell forward as Jeremy rolled to his side. The knife flashed through the air, and Pepe watched in horror as it sunk into Jeremy's shoulder.

There was a mad scramble as both men went for the gun in Jeremy's holster.

A moment later, the night was pierced by a single gunshot.

Pepe stood amidst the commotion, his mind retreating into a quiet—or rather shell-shocked—place. One of the medical examiners rolled Harlan's body over and opened the shirt to reveal a bullet hole, right in the center of what appeared to be a bull's eye tattoo.

Dr. John Harlan, a small town vet, ex US Marine, and Jeremy's psychotic father, was...the Lost Dog Killer.

How had he missed it?

The deep, gravelly words of Chief Roland circled around his head. Roland had told him all about Jeremy's dad, the bar fight in college and the tattoo he was now looking at, covered in blood. His was the vet clinic Jeremy had busted into, and he'd been the one who'd beaten Jeremy for sport.

*Yeah, I was afraid for Jeremy when he was a kid,* Roland had said. *That's why I let him slide so many times. I knew one day one day Jeremy's father was going to kill him.*

Surprised, Pepe had asked, *Did you really think he'd go that far?*

The older man had suddenly looked sad. *Son, I'm pretty sure he's gotten away with it before. Jeremy's mom was murdered...we just couldn't prove it.*

In the end, it had been a decorated war hero's story against a depressed woman with a history of covert drinking, now dead and unable to defend herself.

*And Jeremy?*

According to Chief Roland, there was a good chance the young boy had watched him kill her.

Pepe turned and saw him holding Monica, who, thank the Lord, was slowly coming back to life. An ambulance officer was trying to tend to the many spots on Jeremy's body that were black with blood, but he made it clear he wished to be left with his wife.

Pepe had been convinced such an upbringing could only create a killer, instead, it had forged a warrior. If only he'd been able to see it.

# CHAPTER SIXTY-FOUR

Before now, she hadn't known who he was. She hadn't known about the horrors of his childhood, or the guilt he'd carried for so long. She didn't know the origin of all his scars, or where he went when his eyes closed down, and glassed over. Neither did she know where his endless, unstoppable rage sprung from, or how he managed to focus and refine it from blind fury, into a controlled finger held light against a trigger.

And now, as they sat together at the surprise party he'd thrown for no better reason than to celebrate their love, she looked across the table and realized how lost he once was and now… how found.

# ABOUT THE AUTHOR

Bryan Kennedy is credited as a singer, songwriter, author, playwright, actor, keynote speaker and Spot Life Coach. Possibly best known for the three #1 Garth Brooks hits he penned, the Ole Miss football star has written numerous works. They include two plays, two animated cartoon scripts and two children books in addition to three books for adults. His own musical projects include; "Dis-Connected", "I'm so Jealous of Me", **Life. Love. Laugh** and "Made in the Shade".

An actor at heart, Kennedy landed a leading role in, "The Secret Handshake" starring Kevin Sorbo. Additionally, his play "Toe Roaster" is slated to become a motion picture at the end of 2015. He will star in the acclaimed musical comedy's film adaptation.

To purchase Bryan Kennedy's books visit Createspace.com, the iTunes Bookstore or bryanswebsite.com.

For Kennedy's music visit
cdbaby.com/Artist/BryanKennedy and
itunes.apple.com/us/artist/bryan-kennedy/id1390631.

To view videos of Kennedy's hits visit
youtube.com/user/bryanswebsite?feature=watch.

Contact:
management@bryan-kennedy.com

# Bryan Kennedy

Website:
bryanswebsite.com

Social Media:
facebook.com/bryankennedyfanpage
twitter.com/UnderBryansHat
instagram.com/cowabungaboy

www.ingramcontent.com/pod-product-compliance
Lightning Source LLC
Chambersburg PA
CBHW070925250626

47159CB00009B/3131